Lexi's Choice

by

Linda Apple

Moonlight Mississippi, Book 3

This is a work of fiction. Names, characters, places, and incidents are either the product of the author's imagination or are used fictitiously, and any resemblance to actual persons living or dead, business establishments, events, or locales, is entirely coincidental.

Lexi's Choice

COPYRIGHT © 2022 by Linda Apple

All rights reserved. No part of this book may be used or reproduced in any manner whatsoever without written permission of the author or The Wild Rose Press, Inc. except in the case of brief quotations embodied in critical articles or reviews.
Contact Information: info@thewildrosepress.com

Cover Art by *The Wild Rose Press, Inc.*

The Wild Rose Press, Inc.
PO Box 708
Adams Basin, NY 14410-0708
Visit us at www.thewildrosepress.com

Publishing History
First Edition, 2022
Trade Paperback ISBN 978-1-5092-4103-3
Digital ISBN 978-1-5092-4104-0

Moonlight Mississippi, Book 3
Published in the United States of America

The sun bore down, breaking through the cool spring day. I shifted to the shade of newly furled maple leaves. "Look, we are just going to have to figure out how to live together. I don't know if I can ever be your friend, but this I promise you. I'll try and make your life comfortable. But there are rules you'll have to follow."

"Fair."

"I am in a relationship with Nathan Wolfe." His eyebrows rose. Before he could ask, I said, "Yes. *The* Nathan Wolfe, national news field correspondent. Maybe someday I'll tell you how all that came about. But for now, I do not want you to have any—*any*—contact with him, nor do I want any advice about my relationship with him. He doesn't make it to Moonlight often, but when he does, make yourself scarce. I'm turning the den into your space and having Felix put in a shower. So you'll have plenty of room and we'll both have privacy. You can have the patio in the backyard, and I will use the front porch."

"Thanks, Lex. I really appreciate this. Truly. It's more than I deserve."

Why did he have to be so humble? It made it harder to hate him, so I conjured up my hurt just long enough to harden my heart and enjoy his misery.

Funny thing was? It didn't make my pain ease up one little bit.

Dedication

I dedicate this book
to all the southern women in my life:
especially my mother, Freddie Diehl,
my grandmothers,
Clady Mae Leslie and Molly Bell Lowe,
my aunt, Peggy Grogan,
and my feisty cousin, Cherrell Grogan.

Acknowledgments

Loving gratitude to my husband, Neal Apple, who makes my writing possible, and for his undying support.

Loving thanks to my daughters, Amanda and Olivia, for their support and suggestions.

And many thanks to my critique partners, Ruth Weeks and Chrissy Willis.

Dear Readers,

Many of you have asked when the third book of my Moonlight Mississippi would be available. I began to imagine Lexi's story several months after *Avalee's Gift* was published. In the spring of 2019, I began writing *Lexi's Choice*. I had my first draft done by December. I had every intention of sending the manuscript to the publisher by late spring of 2020.

The year of 2020 was hard on everyone and on businesses. It also stopped me from continuing my work on this book. On January 17th my father passed away. It happened so fast. He was fine on New Year's Day. On the 4th he went to the hospital with breathing problems and passed 13 days later. It isn't known if he had contracted COVID-19. None of us were aware of this virus at that time. Whatever it was, it contributed to his heart failing.

I spent the next four months helping my mother through all the legalities and the business of financial matters. I lived three hours away from her so I spent a lot of time on the road. During this time, I had noticed my mom's mental health changing since my dad's death. I was concerned that she might be developing dementia. Another cause to worry was that she began having trouble holding things with her left hand. Believing she may have had a small stroke she went in for an MRI on July 10th. It was then that she was diagnosed with metastatic brain cancer, lung cancer, (even though she quit smoking twenty years ago) and liver cancer.

I moved her home with me and arranged for in-home Hospice care. My precious momma spent the next two weeks visiting with her grandchildren and great grandchildren, then she made up her mind it was time to go to Heaven and passed three days later on July 31st.

Once again, I spent months closing the book on her life and grieving the loss of both parents. When I felt emotionally strong enough, I sat at my computer and rewrote much of *Lexi's Choice*. I had learned so much. My eyes had been opened to this precious gift called life and also how fleeting it is. So many distractions and stresses rob us of living a full life. I wanted to give a loving warning and hope in this novel for all of you to grasp my gentle reminder about the preciousness of life and loved ones.

I love hearing from you. Please feel free to contact me. My email is: linda@lindaapple.com

Magnolia blooms, sweet tea, and porch swing blessings to you all!

~Linda

Prologue

I stood by the mailbox, staring at the letter in my hand. Why do we do that? Just stare at the letter while wondering what's in it? Why not just tear it open?

Perhaps because I didn't want to know what it contained, and yet, I was dying to know. It was from my ex-husband who, for many years now, has been incarcerated in the Mississippi State Penitentiary for statutory rape. Yep. My educated, well-respected doctor husband impregnated a fifteen-year-old girl, thinking she was a college student. I'm sure her "sweater-puppies" were what clouded his judgment. Problem was, he chose to remain in that hormonal fog.

Memories of that night—on our twenty-eighth anniversary—when he told me about her, still assaulted my soul. Then—THEN—he asked what *we* were going to do. *We*? WE were not going to do anything about her or the baby. No. *I* was going to kick his sorry ass out of our house and out of my life.

I shoved the envelope in the back pocket of my jeans, the appropriate part of my anatomy for his letter, and strode back into the house.

Chapter One

The letter

Fury blazed inside me as I read the letter, re-read it, crumpled it up, then threw it across the room only to retrieve it and read it again. Fisting the paper in my hand, I screamed at the top of my lungs, “Haven’t you put me through enough, Toby Lowe? Now this?”

Thanks to this unwelcomed intrusion into my life, the rest of my afternoon was shot. I glanced at the time. Four-fifteen. Might as well call it a day. I needed wine—no—bourbon. Bourbon with a friend. Molly Kate to be exact. She hated Toby as much as I did. After all, she was the one who held my hand through the whole nightmare from the fallout of his infidelity. Together we would roast him on a spit and have him for dinner. That put a smile on my face as I stabbed every digit of her phone number.

Molly Kate answered on the first ring. Good. “Hey, girl. What’s up?”

“My place. Five-thirty. I have bourbon. You bring food. Oh, and leave your husband at home.”

“Good gracious. What’s got a reindeer up your butt?”

“I’ll tell you when you get here.” I hung up the phone, feeling better. Molly would know what I should do.

Lord, I loved my friends.

****

Molly Kate stared at her phone. What in the world was that all about? She wasn't sure she was up to more drama. Business at her bakery, A Taste of Heaven, had boomed to the point where she was going to have to find another place to expand. This was a problem because in Mayor Campbell's zeal to turn Moonlight into a tourist town, real estate was hard to find. In addition to the bakery, the bed and breakfast she and her husband, Stan, owned, stayed full, thanks to the glowing article in the area's most popular southern magazine.

But whaddya do when your best friend in the world calls yowling like a wounded cat? And to be honest, curiosity was getting the better of her anyway. Curiosity was her one downfall.

She called to her granddaughters. "Lacey? Cherrell?"

Both girls finished serving their customers and then walked over.

"Can y'all close for me tonight? I've got business I gotta see about."

Thank goodness for kin. She didn't feel one whit bad for taking advantage of them. After all, hadn't she changed their muddy diapers when they were babies for what seemed like a lifetime? Didn't she read to them at bedtime until she needed toothpicks to hold her eyes open? Didn't she run behind them at the park until her knees gave out? Yes, to all examples. No, she didn't feel bad at all.

The girls weren't too happy, but after giving them the *grandma* look, they nodded their heads and started messaging on their phones. Cancelling plans, she supposed, and that did give her a miniscule pang of guilt. But Lexi needed her, for crying out loud.

She hurried home to whip up something to take to Lexi's. After tying on her apron, she fisted her hands on her hips and surveyed her kitchen. Now what kind of food to take? Let's see. Lexi obviously had some kind of problem, therefore, the situation called for fat and carbs. Stan said he had mixed up a batch of sausage cheese balls for breakfast at the B&B for the next morning. Perfect. She'd snatch a few of those and pop them in the oven. He wouldn't miss them. That took care of the savory fat and carbs. Now for the sweet carbs. She didn't have enough time to make Lexi's favorite indulgence, orange rolls, but she did have enough time to make her next favorite, chocolate chunk cookies.

She left her kitchen to get the sausage balls from the mansion's kitchen. When she and Stan had purchased a beautiful white antebellum house right before they married, her friends were astounded that they had decided to turn it into a bed and breakfast instead of living there, but it was far too large. The original owner, Mr. Norton, added an addition to the mansion for his parents and connected the buildings with a glass anteroom. She and Stan figured they could live quite comfortably in the three-thousand square foot space, thank you very much.

"Hey, you're home early." Stan dipped his head as a slow smile spread across his face.

"Don't get any ideas." She brushed her lips across his cheek. "Emergency on Washington Avenue."

"Miss Cladie, Avalee, or Lexi?"

"Lexi."

"What's up with her?"

"No idea. But something has her tail in a twist. I'm going to steal some of your sausage balls and make cookies. Oh, and by the way, your presence was not requested."

"Thank God for small favors." Stan made his saddest puppy-eyed face. "But I'll miss you."

Molly Kate slapped at his arm. "Pssh, I know it's poker night." Poker night was a new tradition at the B&B open to both guests and locals alike. "Any takers?"

"Yep, full table."

"Okay, I'll make extra cookies. Will that soothe your hurt feelers?"

"Sounds good." He kissed her cheek. "I'm going to the library and set up for the game."

Molly waved him off and hurried back to her kitchen. While she mixed the dough she wondered, what could be wrong? Her job? Problems with Nate? Nate. Molly nodded her head. That had to be it. Even though Lexi said she and Nate were just friends with benefits, Lex probably really had deeper feelings for him.

Oh brother. Molly rolled her eyes. What should she say? "I never liked the guy," or "You are from two different worlds, I told you it wouldn't work." Even though both statements were true, it wouldn't help saying them to Lex while she was in a snit.

She slid two trays of cookies in the top oven and a few of the sausage balls into the lower one. When the cookies were done, she decided to take a platter to the library, even though the poker game was a couple of hours away. This, at least, would save Stan one detail in his preparations. The library was empty. She noticed, again, the lingering smell of pipe smoke and peppermint. She'd confronted Stan about his smoking many times, but he always insisted it wasn't him. Not that she minded pipe smoke. Actually, she liked it. But not in the mansion. She had a no smoking rule for safety purposes, so it wouldn't be good for guests to find the owner smoking for heaven's sakes. If he wanted to smoke, he could do it at home.

Men. Go figure.

Chapter Two

Sometimes, my friends show their love by telling me what I don't want to hear.

As usual, Molly Kate didn't bother knocking when she got to my house. She just swung open the door and marched inside, balancing bags on either arm.

"Okay, Lex. I've got the food. You'd better have drinks ready *and* an explanation of what the heck is going on."

I gave her a bourbon and soda, then shoved the crumpled letter in her other hand. "Read this." I grabbed platters for the food. "Aloud." I set the food on the coffee table while MK rummaged through her purse for her readers. She sat on the couch and cleared her throat. I settled in next to her and took a slug from my glass.

MK looked at me, then at the letter and began:

"Dear Lexi,

I'll bet I'm the last person you ever expected to hear from. Now, before you throw this in the trash, please hear me out. I've had a lot of time these past six years to reflect on my idiotic mistake."

Lexi threw up her hands. "How do you like that? Mistake. *Mistake?* Mis-adding the figures in my checkbook is a mistake. Adding salt to my cake instead of sugar is a mistake." She held up her index finger and waggled it back and forth. "*This* was *no* mistake. It was a *decision*. A very stupid, selfish, decision."

"Amen, sister. You got that right." Molly Kate scanned the letter and after finding her place returned to reading:

"These years have not been kind, not just because of the conditions of my living, but the regret that haunts me every day. Lexi, I had so much to live for. My career, my freedom...you. Especially you. I would have never made it through school or the grueling hours to get to where I was and what did I do? I gave it up because some cute girl made this balding, south-of-middle-age man feel young again."

Molly looked up from the letter. "Well, la-de-da. Hand me a sausage ball."

I passed her the platter.

She popped one in her mouth. "Okay, now where was I? *Feel young again...*" After washing the snack down with a swig from her glass, she continued, reading aloud, "*My reason for writing is that due to a health issue, I've been given the opportunity to receive a compassionate release. Not paroled but held as house arrest. You know, the whole ankle bracelet thing. The problem is that I need a house to be held in. As you know, I have no family, and fewer friends who would welcome me as a semi-permanent guest in their home. The only home I have owned is ours...now yours. So, the only person I can appeal to is you. Lexi, you are my only hope."*

MK snorted. "You gotta be kidding me."

"I know. But read on." I stood to refill our glasses.

"Now before you wad this letter up and throw it away..."

I handed MK her glass. "And that is exactly what I did. He knows me well."

"I'm about to." Molly took a drink. *"...hear me out. The reason I'm given this chance is, well, I'm dying. Lung cancer. It's kind of funny in a way. I smoked all the way through medical school and gave it up when I began my practice because it was unhealthy and a bad example for my patients. After all, I was in the health profession and didn't want to be hypocritical. But here in prison I took it up again and even with all the signs, like shortness of breath, some chest pain, I chose to ignore them. I diagnosed myself as having mild asthma and angina. And now, well, it's too late.*

Molly's head shot up and her gaze met mine. "Good Lord."

A pent-up sigh escaped me. "I know."

She went back to reading, *"I could have surgery, chemo, and all of that. But in the long run, it will only give me a few more months of pain. I'm choosing quality of life over treatments. Lex, I know I have no right to your mercy or your home, but I don't want to die in prison. If you will let me stay until it's necessary for me to go to hospice, I will, to the best of my ability, do all I can to make up to you for all the pain I've caused.*

"I promise, I won't be a burden. For now, except for some shortness of breath, I feel pretty good. The doc says I have maybe a year, perhaps a little longer. But when I start needing care, I'll go to hospice.

"If you agree, or even if you don't, you can reach me at the address on the envelope. Should you agree, I will put you in contact with the right persons.

All my love, Toby."

"Well, I'll be." Molly handed me the letter. "So what are you going to do?"

I flopped back on the couch. "I don't know. I want to tell him to rot in hell." Rolling my head toward her, I sighed. "But you know I can't."

"But for him to live with you? What about Nate?" Molly reached for a cookie. "How about some coffee with these cookies?"

"Coming right up." I stood and gathered our glasses and empty sausage ball platter. "I'll keep seeing Nate. Might be good for Toby to see I've moved on. At least someone finds me desirable."

I slogged to the kitchen, and Molly Kate called, "Where will you put him?"

That thought hadn't crossed my mind yet. I put a pod in my handy-dandy single cup maker and soon the aroma of coffee filled the kitchen. I wish coffee tasted as good as it smelled while brewing. Returning to the living room, I handed MK a mug. "I have two guest rooms upstairs."

"Thanks." Molly took a sip then arched an eyebrow and peered at me with her cat-green eyes. "But when he gets to where he can't climb stairs, then what?"

"You think I ought to give him *my* room?" Agitated, I took a gulp of coffee, burning my tongue and all the way down my throat. I sucked in air. "Ow. Darn it!"

"No, but you do have the den off the kitchen and a half-bath.

"But my fireplace…"

"You mean the one you never use?"

I grabbed a cookie and shoved half of it in my

mouth. So, so, good. "Well, if you put it that way, I guess the den would work. But he'd have to use my shower when he's in no condition to climb the stairs. I don't know how I feel about that."

"You'd just have to work out a schedule." An evil grin spread on MK's face. "And when Nate uses it…"

I slapped at her arm. "Oh, stop it."

"Okay, but seriously, I'll bet Felix can add a small shower in the den's bathroom."

"Yeah, he probably could."

I nibbled on another cookie as the looming reality of how my whole life was about to be turned upside down shrouded me. Toby wouldn't be the only prisoner in my home. I would be too.

"So what should I do, Molly Kate?"

"Well, if it were me, I'd tell him to kiss the south end of a north-bound mule. And then I'd let him stay."

"Really?"

"For heaven's sakes. The man is dying." She patted my shoulder. "Now go and write that letter telling him to kiss your ass. Then tell him he can stay."

"I'll think on it. More coffee?"

"No girl, I gotta get back to Stan-My-Man."

"Okay." Standing, I held my arms out to her. "Thanks for coming over."

MK gave me one of her famous bear hugs. "Love you."

"Love you back."

When she left, I wandered around the room, still too upset to settle anywhere. I had hoped this heart-to-heart with my friend would help. It sorta did, but not really. Sure, it would feel good telling Toby what he could do with his sorry self, but that darned angel on my shoulder kept telling me to do the right thing.

I decided to visit Miss Cladie the next morning, even though I knew, without a doubt, what *she* would say. For now, I just wanted a hot bath and bed.

****

Sometime just before dawn a rumble of thunder broke through my thin facade of sleep. I checked the clock for the fourth time. Five-thirty. My body felt like it had been massaged with horse hooves. What an awful night. I dreamed that Toby and I had a baby girl. She had red hair like mine, blue eyes like his. I named her Anna. Even in my dream, I could feel my intense love for her.

Then, in a split second, Toby grabbed her from my arms and thrust her toward his teenaged lover, declaring, "You aren't Anna's mother." He snaked his arm around the girl. "She is."

His lover smirked while clutching Anna, who cried as she reached her little hands for me. I woke, sobbing for my child. The child I never had. Needless to say, after that, sleep never came.

Giving up, I shoved the quilt back and sat up. There was no sense in trying to sleep. A flash of light pierced through my slatted window shade and a thunderous crack quickly followed. Looked like we were in for quite a storm. I slipped out of bed and hurried to the kitchen to make coffee just in case the power went out. A night of tossing and turning needed to be followed with coffee—lots of coffee.

I hugged my mug to my chest and opened the front door to breathe in the cool, moist, dawn. Thankfully, my porch was deep and covered, so I decided to sit on my swing and sort out all the emotions tangled up in my mind. I always thought better outside. For a long time, I swayed back and forth while remembering my dream. Tears gathered and slid down my cheeks. Why? Why am I in this position where I really have no moral choice but to let him back in my life? Up until now things were good. I liked my job and my work with Sid. Nate was a real plus, I mean, who would have thought I'd be dating a news god? My friends were my rock, my anchor. Then like a blemish on the end of my nose, Toby pops up. Ugly and unwanted.

The storm passed and a cardinal ventured out in the blue-gray light and trilled his song. I tossed my cold coffee over the porch rail, stood, and stretched before walking to the sidewalk to see if Miss Cladie's light was on. It was. Even though I knew what she would say, I needed her motherly assurance—and her hot biscuits.

The aroma of coffee met me at Miss Cladie's kitchen door. For most, it would be way too early for a visit. But not for Miss Cladie. That blessed soul's door was always open.

I rapped lightly, opened the door, and called, "Knock, knock?"

Miss Cladie turned from taking the biscuits out of the oven.

"Honey, get yourself in here."

I took my seat at her little drop-leaf table that stood against the wall that was decorated with at least a dozen smiling plaster of Paris fruits and vegetables. These smiling bananas and laughing tomatoes had hung there for as long as I could remember.

After setting the pan on the counter, she wiped her hands on her apron and walked over with outstretched arms. "What brings you here so early?"

"Miss Cladie, I need some advice. Like right now." I brought out the crumpled letter and pressed it into her hand. "Read this."

"I will, but first, sit down and have a bite to eat."

She'd get no argument from me. In no time I was enjoying a biscuit slathered in butter and fig preserves, as well as a slice of fried ham, and coffee.

Coffee mug in hand, Miss Cladie joined me at the table, took out her glasses, and began to read. After she read down a few lines, her hand went to her chest. "Mercy Lord." She continued without looking up, alternately shaking her head, and blessing his heart.

Bless his heart indeed. I scarfed down the rest of my biscuit and buttered another.

When she finally looked up, I said, "Well?"

"God love him, that is the most pitiful situation I've heard of in a long time."

"Pitiful? He made that bed and now he's lying in it."

Miss Cladie reached out and patted my hand. "Don't we all?"

I knew it. Here it came…the truth I didn't want to hear. "So, what do I do?"

"I think you already know that."

"I knew that's what you'd say." Her Swiss chalet coo-coo clock ticked the seconds while I tried to stop the words demanding release, but I couldn't and blurted out, "I don't want him there. And God help me, but I hate him. I don't need to be reminded of my humiliation and his rejection every blessed day. Besides, I have a life now. I have Nate and I don't want Toby disrupting my life."

Miss Cladie held up her hand. "I understand. But it is always better to choose on the side of compassion. Think about it, Nate isn't here that often, now is he? And I'm sure he would understand your situation. So just for a moment, let's say that you did let him move in with you. Where would you put him?"

I slapped the table. "That's another thing. My guest rooms are upstairs. There will be a time when he can't climb the stairs and I'm sure as heck not moving out of my room."

Miss Cladie didn't say a word. She knew the power of silence. Her conversation pauses were so powerful they left me babbling like a fool.

"Molly did mention the den off the kitchen and said Felix could install a small shower…but…"

"That's a good idea."

"But my fireplace?"

"You mean the one you never use?" Darned it, that's what Molly had said.

"Maybe," Miss Cladie reached across the table to pat my hand, "the good Lord wants him in your face to help you get free of him."

"Free?" What was she saying? I was free of him when he was locked up and out of my life.

"Honey, you have chained yourself to your pain. Think about it. After all these years and you still suffer. Think of how we always move in the direction of our focus. Yours is Toby's betrayal and all you lost while trying to be the perfect wife. You are letting your past interfere with your present."

I looked up from my cup and studied her face. "How do you figure that?"

"Sugar, I've known you all your life. Since Toby's

betrayal I've watched you change. Under all that sarcasm is a hurt and angry woman. You are so full of fear and mistrust that you cannot even commit to anyone else no matter how much you like him."

"That's not true."

But it was.

"Lexi, honey, you are going to have to forgive him."

"I try, Miss Cladie, I do. But about the time I think I have, something reminds me of him and I get so angry all over again." I blew out a breath. "Doesn't it say somewhere in the Bible that we have to forgive and forget? Well, I can't forgive because I can't forget."

Miss Cladie shook her head. "Baby, it doesn't say that at all. You can forgive without forgetting." She laid her hand on my arm. "Besides, God created our minds to always remember." A sly smile spread between her wrinkled cheeks. "That is, at least until you get around eighty. You have a few years yet."

Sighing, I stood, walked to the sink, and placed my cup on the counter beside it. I stared at the little China cat with tiny kittens on Miss Cladie's windowsill. "I wish I could forget."

"So, the question remains, and I think you know the answer. Are you going to let him move back in?"

Everything in me screamed, "NO! NOT FAIR!"

But I heard myself say, "Probably so."

Chapter Three

Forget fences. Rules make better neighbors.

On the three-hour drive, in the sultry heat of July, I second guessed my decision all the way to the Mississippi Department of Corrections. I still hadn't summoned the courage to let Nathan know what I was doing. What would he say? With him there was no telling. But no matter. Here I am, waiting for Toby to walk through the door—a prisoner in my custody.

How ironic. One of our wedding pictures was of me holding a key to the fuzzy handcuffs he wore behind his back. If it wasn't so pitiful, I might even chuckle.

The authorities briefed me on the conditions of his house-arrest. He had to wear an ankle monitor. Fortunately, the judge was lenient about approved activities. In other words, I hadn't been reduced to a babysitter. His curfew began at 9 p.m. and ended at 7 a.m. the next morning. I could see a lot of evenings at Molly Kate's in my future.

I waited for what seemed like forever. Finally, the door to the lobby opened and Toby walked through. I hadn't seen him in six years, so really, I had no idea what to expect, but what I saw was, well, let's just say even *my* imagination could never have envisioned the way he looked. My former potbellied, six-foot-one ex, had to have lost forty pounds. His skin was loose and sallow. His horseshoe of sandy-blond hair had grown thinner. The only part of him I recognized were his bright blue eyes. They still pierced. I started to speak, but there were no words. A rarity. The Sahara Dessert couldn't have been as dry as my mouth.

Finally, he spoke. "Hi, Lex."

"Hi."

Anger, resentment, regret, hate, all clamored for control, but from somewhere deep in my soul the tiniest spark of affection still demanded to be recognized.

"Are you ready?" Stupid question, but I really didn't know what to say.

"Yes."

He literally had only what was on his back and one small bag. I guessed it contained toiletry items and a change of clothes. I hoped so, because what I hadn't thrown out the door when I kicked him out had gone to Goodwill. I sighed. He'd have to go clothes shopping, and I'd probably be the one buying them.

Darned his sorry hide.

An emotional stew bubbled inside of me. Love, hate, pity, hard-heartedness, the desire to forgive, the inability to forget. Until now, I thought I was a good person, but now I wasn't so sure.

When we got in the car, Toby slumped in the passenger seat and stared at his shoes like a guilty teenager about to be grounded. The proverbial elephant sat firmly ensconced between us and practically sucked the air out of the car. I had no words. My brain hurt from the effort of trying to think of something—anything—to break the weight of silence.

To my relief, he broke the ice. "Feels weird, doesn't it?"

Weird? Tears stung my eyes. I couldn't believe it still hurt so bad. But he would not see me cry. Never again. I didn't say anything. Instead, I stared ahead and willed my eyes to dry.

"Lex, I don't want to die with you still hating me. What will it take for you to forgive me?"

What would it take? I honestly didn't know. He paid a debt. Now he was dying. Wasn't that enough?

No.

I wanted back the years I had wasted loving him. I wanted children—a happy family instead of the social-climbing partnership that we had created. Deep regret forced the tears I had fought back to stream down my cheeks.

"Talk to me." He put his hand on my shoulder. "Scream at me if it helps."

"What are you doing?" I jerked away so hard the car swerved. "Don't ever touch me again."

He hadn't touched me since the night he told me about his affair. Memories of love pats conflicted with my imagination of his stroking her skin. My chest throbbed as if I were at the bottom of Moonlight Lake desperate for air. No. There would be *no* touching. That ship had sailed.

We approached the Moonlight National Forest. On a whim, I whipped the car in the entrance and parked at a picnic table well away from anyone who might overhear me should I start screaming like a banshee.

"Get out."

His face went blank. "What?"

"I said get out. We are going to shoot this elephant between us before we walk into *my* house, cause I can't live with it every blessed day of my life."

He held his hands up. “All right, all right.”

We sat on top of a concrete picnic table. I stayed silent while gathering my thoughts. He hung his head and stared at his clamped hands.

Where to begin? I mean, what was there to say that hadn’t been said well over a hundred times already since the day I’d first been told about his adultery with a minor. What could I say about his making a baby with a baby?

I studied his face, now drawn and so old looking. He had paid the price for his decision. But I had too, hadn’t I? It wasn’t fair. I was the faithful one after all.

Miss Cladie said to forgive, but how? I couldn’t. All I knew to do was push it down—way down—far away from my mind.

I cleared my throat. “Toby, I honestly don’t know if I can ever forgive and forget.”

He studied the ground and nodded his head.

The struggle to go against my bitterness and do what was right was unbearable. I couldn’t look at him when I said, “But I’ll try.”

“Thanks, Lex. I know I don’t deserve it. If I could change things I would.” He sighed and looked up into the sky, staring at the clouds. “Sitting in that prison I often imagined being able to go back in time and talk to the man I was, to warn him that he was about to lose everything. The love of his life, his home, freedom, career, all respect.

He turned to me. “Hell, I can’t even live within a mile of a school because I’m a registered sex offender.”

“I’m well aware of that. It just so happens that a single father, AJ, and his daughter, Junie, have moved into Jema’s house. I had to tell AJ about you.”

"Oh god. I'm so damned sorry."

The sun bore down, breaking through the cool spring day. I shifted to the shade of newly furled maple leaves. "Look, we are just going to have to figure out how to live together. I don't know if I can ever be your friend, but this I promise you. I'll try and make your life comfortable. But there are rules you'll have to follow."

"Fair."

"I am in a relationship with Nathan Wolfe." His eyebrows rose. Before he could ask, I said, "Yes. *The* Nathan Wolfe, national news field correspondent. Maybe someday I'll tell you how all that came about. But for now, I do not want you to have any—*any*—contact with him, nor do I want any advice about my relationship with him. He doesn't make it to Moonlight often, but when he does, make yourself scarce. I'm turning the den into your space and having Felix put in a shower. So, you'll have plenty of room and we'll both have privacy. You can have the patio in the backyard, and I will use the front porch."

"Thanks, Lex. I really appreciate this. Truly. It's more than I deserve."

Why did he have to be so humble? It made it harder to hate him, so I conjured up my hurt just long enough to harden my heart and enjoy his misery.

Funny thing was? It didn't make my pain ease up one little bit.

****

Toby stared at his feet while Lexi reminded him of what a loser—a jerk—an absolute ass—he had been. Sad thing was, she was right on all counts. Honestly? If he'd had another choice, she would have been the last person he'd have called because he knew this would cause her pain. But he had no one. Crawling back to her on his hands and knees was another blow to his nearly non-existent pride.

Every now and then he'd glance up at her. Age had been kind. She still had fiery red hair, except for the white roots peeking at her temple. She still moved quick and easy like a teen. Except for a few laugh lines around her eyes, her smooth skin showed no signs of wrinkles. He fought the urge to put his arms around her, draw her close, and kiss her. Just to feel her body next to his one last time.

What a fool. A fool! If he hadn't been such a gullible, full-of-himself moron, they'd still be together having the time of their lives. They would have traveled to Europe, several times. Heck, they might have even bought a home there. And why not? There was nothing in Moonlight to keep them there. No children.

A sinking feeling overwhelmed him. Should he tell her? The secret he'd kept from her all the years they were married weighed especially heavy on him. But it was best for him to hold those cards close. Her feelings were still too raw. No need to make them worse.

He repositioned himself on the concrete picnic table. He needed a cigarette. Ironic, wasn't it? Here he was a medical doctor dying of lung cancer because he smoked. Even though he'd quit smoking after medical school, sheer boredom in prison tempted him to take it up again. And bam. Cancer. Why him? Years ago, while still practicing medicine, he had a patient who had smoked since the age of fifteen. That guy lived into his nineties.

Life. So unpredictable.

When Lexi mentioned Nathan Wolfe, he didn't think he'd heard her right. *The Nathan Wolfe?* When? How? She made it clear those questions were off limits, but still, how? Then again, he didn't doubt anything she could do. That woman had worked wonders for his practice and standing in the community. She could do anything.

He could sum himself up in three words, stupid, stupid, and stupid.

****

"Toby? Did you hear me?"

He blinked, trying to return from his thoughts to the present. "What was that?"

"That just figures. Nothing changes." She threw back her head and huffed. "You didn't hear a word I said."

"I did. I promise. You said that I'm a jerk, I'll live in the den, Nathan Wolfe is off limits." He gave a half chuckle. "Just a lot to take in. I'm still trying to get used to being on the other side of the razor-topped fence."

Lexi levered off the table. "Then let's go."

On the way home, Toby couldn't help but rubberneck all around him. "Man, this place has changed. When did it get to be such a tourist spot?"

"Since Sid Campbell became mayor. He's done a lot for this town." Lexi shrugged a shoulder. "I'm his new PR person. We make a good team."

"I don't doubt it. I've seen you in action. We were once a team, remember?"

"Don't even go there, Toby Lowe." Her mouth pressed into a line and her knuckles grew white on the steering wheel.

He could see the next few weeks were going to be

dicey while he learned to navigate her emotions and rules.

She'd had her say and laid down her rules. He knew he really didn't have a right to say anything, even so, he still had to make some things clear as well.

"Lex, look. I'm sorry. The truth is, I don't know how to make up for what I did. But please give me some slack. I've been penned up for a long time. We haven't spoken a word in six years. You are hurt. I get that. No matter how hard I try not to, I'm still going to make mistakes. When I do, you have to know that I'm not trying to hurt you. Please. Bear with me until I find some footing."

She cut her eyes at him then back to the road. "I guess we both need to find our footing." A moment passed and she blew out a breath. "I'll try."

They pulled onto the driveway and Toby took it all in. Once again, regret gnawed at him. Something, he supposed, he would have to live with the rest of his short life.

Chapter Four

Adjustments and other annoying things.

When I cut the engine, Toby stared at the house like he'd never seen it before. Sure, I'd made some improvements like enlarging the front porch, but for the most part, it was the same as when he left.

Maybe he was remembering the night of our anniversary when he told me he had impregnated a teenager. Or finding his clothes on the front lawn. Maybe he remembers trying his key in the lock. The lock that had been changed.

Toby blinked and tears rolled down his cheeks.

A spark of pity ignited, but I refused to let it flame. Instead I got out of the car, swung my arm toward the door, and said, "You know the way."

He nodded, gathered his stuff and ambled to the den.

Later in the evening I fixed a bourbon and seltzer, then headed to my porch swing. Toby stayed in his room, which was a good thing. I'd grown accustomed to living alone and I liked it—mostly. Oh, there were those times that I missed comfortable evening conversations and morning chats over coffee. Like now. On this swing. Nestled next to a warm body, rocking back and forth, staring at the twilight sky. No expectations. No talking. Simply being.

In the gauze of dusk, fireflies flashed in my yard. Summer still burned and would do so for at least two more months until fall nudged it out. I sipped my bourbon and wondered where this change of situations would take me. Probably to a place I didn't want to go. Forget sipping. I took a gulp of my drink. *Damn that Toby.*

My imagination was well on its way into a feverish fit when my phone rang.

Nathan.

Good. I needed a sexy call from my two-year national-news-reporter-god crush. Funny how our relationship came about. He was Avalee's friend who she met while living in New York City. So, when I tried to get my column syndicated, she suggested I contact him for an opinion. He slammed my article, but gave me good advice. After I got over my hurt feelings, we hit it off and have been together ever since.

"Hi there!" I tried to disguise my crumbling mental state. "How are you?"

"Hi, beautiful. I'm good. I was just thinking about you and wanted to connect. How are you?"

Sighing I said, "I've been better."

"What's up?" Nate's voice sounded concerned.

I went through the whole Toby story. It surprised me how much better I felt talking to a man about this, seeing how they are all on a planet of their own.

"How about me coming down for a visit?"

This suggestion made me bolt upright. "Would you? Oh, Nate, that would be wonderful."

"I'll check my schedule and figure out a time I can head that way. Do I need to get a hotel room?"

"NO." My intensity embarrassed me. "I mean, no,

it isn't necessary. I've told Toby about you and that I didn't want him interfering in my life in any way, shape, or form. I'll tell him you are coming and to stay scarce. He has the entire den to himself. The only place we might bump into him is in the kitchen."

"Well, we'll talk about it when I get there. I'll make travel arrangements and send them to you."

"Make it as soon as possible. I can hardly wait to see you."

"Same here. Night, beautiful."

"Night, sugar."

"I love it when you talk southernese to me."

"Anything for my Yankee."

"Anything?"

"Come on down, hon, and find out."

We hung up and I jiggled the ice in my glass. A visit from Nate. Just the ticket. At least, for now, I could hang on to normal with my fingertips. But, just like summer, I would be forced to change into a new season, kicking and screaming the whole way.

****

My phone woke me from a restless sleep. I pushed the hair out of my eyes and checked the time. Eight-thirty? Lord have mercy, late for work—again. The incessant ringing brought me back to the present. "Hello?"

"Did I wake you? Wait…lemme guess. I did." Molly Kate sniggered. "And you probably think that you're late for work."

"I am and my boss's tighty-whities are probably in a bunch."

"Shug, it's Saturday and how do *you* know what kind of underwear he wears?"

"A guess. He's always so uptight." I sat up, relieved it was Saturday and annoyed that MK woke me. "What's up?"

"I just wanted to see how yesterday went."

"Yesterday?" My brain still felt thick with sleep.

"Toby…duh?"

It all came crashing down on me. Toby. In my house. "Oh, yeah. Okay, I guess."

"Where is he now?

"I have no idea. I haven't seen him since we came home."

"Well, get some clothes on. I'm coming over for coffee and bringing scones."

"Look, I don't think that's a good idea…"

"See you in a few. Ta-ta!"

"…wait, Mk?" The line went dead. I sighed and dragged my body to the bathroom. I noticed the hint of coffee aroma. Huh? How? Oh. Toby. I wasn't used to waking up with a man in the house. I glanced in the mirror. My hair stood out like I'd licked a live electrical wire and I had panda-eyes from sleeping in my mascara. Shoot. Until yesterday I could go to the kitchen naked if I wanted. Now I felt like I had to look presentable and darned it all, I wanted coffee now. But nooo, I had to wash my face and brush my hair and put on something that wasn't see through.

I could slap that man into next week.

Toby sat at the small dinette sipping coffee and staring out the window when I walked in. "Morning, Lex."

I didn't say anything. Instead, I went straight for the coffee. My cup was full of hot water. What tha?

"I warmed your cup up for you."

"Thanks." I remembered doing that for him when we were married. I popped in the pod and waited.

"I made a fresh pot. You don't have to make a single cup."

"How long ago?"

"About thirty minutes."

"Too long." I stirred sugar and cream in my freshly made cup and noticed Toby sat perched in my spot. He patted the chair next to him. "Have a seat and let's have another talk."

"Sorry, but it's way too early for that. I'm going to the swing. Maybe we can talk after my fourth or fifth cup."

"Oh yeah, I'd forgotten your routine. It's been a while."

On the inside I said, "Not long enough." But on the outside, I said, "Yep, it has." The screen door slammed behind me as I shuffled to my swing to sulk.

****

Toby's gaze followed Lexi as she sashayed away. She was still one fine woman. Why didn't he appreciate her when he'd had the chance? And now some super news star was probably appreciating *all* her fine qualities. At least that's what it sounded like to him yesterday evening. He didn't mean to eavesdrop, but the window was open, and he just happened to be in the kitchen.

She didn't sound like she was in love, but she obviously liked the guy. Of that he was certain, and it bothered him. He knew he didn't have a right to be jealous, but he was. It's not like he thought he could move in and pick up where they left off before the *other woman* event. Toby mentally corrected himself, *other girl.*

Claire was his undoing. How was he to know she was a junior in high school? Those double Ds in that tight Ole Miss tee shirt, which he found out later was her *sister's* shirt, certainly convinced him that when the girl said she was a junior that she meant in college, not high school. And for the record, she didn't clarify his misperception either.

He still shuddered when he remembered how the police arrested him in broad daylight for statutory rape. The girl was pregnant and named him as the father. He denied it, of course. After all, due to an infection he was told he was more than likely sterile. If he did sire a child, it would be a bit of a miracle. He'd put off telling Lexi this bit of information, because, who knew? Miracles happened, didn't they? Truth was, it hurt his stupid manly pride to be sterile. Lexi wanted kids. He wanted Lexi. If she had known he couldn't give her kids, it would have changed their relationship. His reasoning was selfish. He knew that now. To be completely honest, he knew it then too, but wouldn't admit it to himself.

When the baby girl was born, he wondered. *Is she my child? Is this my miracle?*

He got his answer. Eventually, Claire's guilty conscience won out and she admitted to him that the child wasn't his after all. No miracle had taken place. And even though the child wasn't his, he was still guilty of having sex with a minor. Nothing changed the fact that he must serve his time.

At least he could be absolved from Lexi's accusation about him denying her children. And when he gathered his courage, he'd tell her the truth.

The doorbell rang, drawing him back into the present. He answered the door and there stood Molly Kate.

"Why, hello, Toby. You look like crap."

"Nice to see you again, too, Molly Kate." He never had to wonder what Molly Kate was thinking. "Lexi's in the shower."

She pushed the door open and slipped by him carrying something on a plate. "She knows I'm coming over. Do you have any coffee made?"

He shut the door behind her. "Come on in."

Molly picked up the carafe and poured out the remaining dregs of coffee. After filling the pot with water, she spooned coffee into the filter and pressed *brew*. Then she turned to him and leaned against the counter. "Well, how does it feel to be back home?"

"Strange." He couldn't think of a better word. "Like a coma patient who wakes up after six years and everything's changed, but still familiar.

"I hope that little gal was worth the coma." Molly took the foil off the scones and held the plate up to him. "Have one. Lord knows you need a little meat on those bones."

He took one. "I wouldn't recommend the prison's weight-loss program. Not to mention the big C."

Molly Kate put her hand on his arm. "Look, Toby. Miracles happen. Let's hope for one, okay?"

He held his scone up in a toast. "Here's to hoping." He poured himself a fresh cup of coffee. "And let's hope Lexi comes out fast. She doesn't like her coffee any older than ten minutes."

"I'll handle her."

"Okay, then. I'll just go back to my den so you gals

can tear me apart."

"I like an understanding man." Molly Kate winked. "Get ready for your ears to burn like fire."

"Is the fire extinguisher where it used to be?"

"Not sure, but I can toss some cold water your way."

He smiled. With thoughts of Lexi in the shower stirring in his imagination, he could probably use a splash.

****

When I stepped out of my room, I heard MK and Toby talking. I really didn't want to deal with him, so I waited until he left, then waited a little longer in case he forgot something.

Molly stuck her head in my room. "Coast is clear. You can come out of hiding now."

I sighed. "It's like I'm a prisoner in my own house."

She took my hand. "Come on. I have a scone with your name on it and fresh coffee."

"Sounds good." I glanced toward the den to make sure the door was firmly closed. "Let's eat on the porch."

"Lord, girl. It's too hot." She slapped her hand in the air toward Toby's door. "He won't come out."

As soon as we sat at the kitchen table, Molly fixed me with her keen eyes. "Honey, you're gonna have to stop this pussy-footing around. She jabbed the pointy end of her scone at me. "This is your house." Jab. "Your rules." Jab. "Your life." Jab. "What you are doing for that jerk is above and beyond what most women would do."

I buttered my scone and bit into the tender bread.

Cinnamon-pecan with buttercream frosting. Lord, it just didn't get any better than this, unless, of course, it was one of her orange rolls.

"You're right, MK. It's all so weird though." I wiped a bit of frosting off my plate with my pinky and popped it in my mouth. "I suppose we will adjust. On a happier note, guess who's coming to visit soon"

Molly's eyebrows arched. "Nate?"

"Yep."

A jaunty smile played across her lips. "Want me to babysit Toby at the B&B?"

I thought for a minute about her offer. When Molly Kate and her husband bought the old Norton mansion, I was a little jealous. I'd dreamed of owning it since childhood. But their turning it into a B & B had been pretty darned handy.

"Tempting, but no. You're right, MK. I've been trying to adjust to him being back in my home. *He* is the one who needs to adjust." With that declaration, I popped the last bite of scone in my mouth and clapped the crumbs off my hands.

"When's he coming?"

"Not sure. He's supposed to have *his people* call *my people.* I smiled. In other words, me."

"Vince will be happy to see his man-crush."

Molly's words couldn't be truer. Vince, the editor of our local paper, as well as my boss, like bragging rights to his acquaintance with a national news field correspondent.

"Yep, and I plan to use that crush to full advantage."

My Audubon bird clock tweeted 10:00. Molly Kate jumped and put her hand to her chest. "Lord, I hate your clock."

"What do you have against robins?"

"I love robins as long as they are outside where they are supposed to be."

"Well, that robin is telling me I need to meet the mayor in an hour. We are brainstorming about new venues for Moonlight. Maybe appeal to the conference crowd, like motivational speakers, writers, new businesses."

Molly stood. "You and Sid get together a lot these days. You should drop Nate and snatch Sid up."

"Now, MK. Let's not go there."

Molly Kate just shrugged her shoulders. "Well, he's a free man now."

"I know. Can you believe his ex's nerve? After disappearing for what? Seven years? She just planned on waltzing back into the family after that rich guy she ran off with dumped her?"

"Why didn't he divorce her years ago? She abandoned them."

I picked up our plates and walked to the sink. "Well, at first, he was really worried that something had happened to her. But after a couple of years and several thousand dollars later, he learned she ran off with some rich guy. He started the proceedings but couldn't get an address to send her a summons. Even her mother had no idea, or so she said. And, our judge, for some weird reason, wouldn't allow Sid to file a motion to serve by publication. He finally found a good lawyer though and dumped that witch."

"What a waste of a good man." Molly Kate snapped her fingers. "You know? It's time for a Whine Wednesday."

Before our little sisterhood went to the four winds, Avalee, Jema, Molly Kate and I would meet once a month for wine and to whine. This was the only day of the month we allowed ourselves to gripe to our hearts' content. All the rest of the time when we were tempted to complain to others, we would write our complaint down and save it for the appointed Wednesday. We also had Martini Mondays where the only thing we were allowed to do was laugh until tears ran down our legs.

Molly frowned. "It'll be just the two of us though."

"Can't we Zoom?"

"Maybe. I'll check the time differences. Gotta go. Love ya." She opened the front door and pushed the screen door with her hip. "Bye now."

I hoped Ava and Jema were at a place where we could Zoom or even Facetime our meeting. The thought of getting back into the flow of normal felt good. Just as I relaxed and started to hum while straightening the kitchen the den door opened and out stepped Toby. My spirits sank.

So much for normal.

****

Toby stood at the door of the kitchen and watched Lexi a moment before entering. She knew he was there. He knew she knew. And he knew she was pretending not to know. So, this was how it was going to be. Games. And while that might be fine for those who think they have years to live, he knew he didn't. So, he might as well plunge on in.

"Can we talk?"

She slapped the towel on the counter and kept her back to him. "I really don't have anything more to say other than I'm not interested in what you have to say."

Irritation rose inside him. She was just being stubborn. “I heard you talking to that Nathan guy last night.”

She whirled around. “You eavesdropped? Why you—”

“Lex, I just came into the kitchen for a glass of tea and the windows were open. You aren’t exactly known for having a soft voice.” He paused, then said, “You know, whatever baggage you have from me will just be carried into a relationship with him.”

“Leave Nate out of this. He’s just a friend.”

“I’m assuming this is a friendship with benefits.”

Lexi’s ears turned cherry red. “Assume what you like you sorry S.O.B. It’s really none of your business.”

“Are you sleeping with him?” He knew he was pushing the limits, but he had to know.

She fixed him with a steely glare. “Do you hear yourself? What a hypocrite. Like I said, it is none of your business.” She stared at him a moment longer and left the room.

Man, he knew she could be hard, but time had turned her heart to stone. When it came to him anyway. She wasn’t always like that though. When he first met her in college, she was a fun-loving girl whose laugh rose up like gleeful bubbles. She was kind, generous, and quick to offer help when needed.

The first time he saw her five-foot-three frame, red hair, and hazel eyes that were sometimes green and other times brown, he thought of her as an Irish sprite. And oh, what she could do with her body. It was something men dreamed about. Something that Nathan character was probably dreaming about now.

That old saying, *you don’t know what you’ve got*

till it's gone, held truer for him than anyone else. He'd taken Lexi for granted. What had he been thinking when Claire bared her naked breasts in a text and invited him to enjoy her charms? He went crazy, that's what. Wouldn't every man? But after he enjoyed those charms, he felt empty. Aloof. Although his needs had been satisfied, something was missing.

One of the many lessons in this whole fiasco? There is more to sex than the meeting of bodies. He and Lexi came together body and *soul.* Something he'd realized too late.

He stood and ambled to his room. He needed someone to talk to, someone to listen with compassion, to offer guidance. But who? Immediately he knew. He left a note for Lexi, walked out the door and up the street to Miss Cladie's.

****

All the way home Molly Kate studied the change she'd seen in Lexi since Toby's out-of-the-blue request. Lexi, her vivacious, sassy, impulsive, friend, had turned into a drooping flower. How dare that man invade Lex's garden like a noxious weed—again. Hadn't she been through enough with him? About the time Lexi was in her prime, here he was again strangling the life out of her.

Molly hit her steering wheel. "Well, Mr. Can't-Keep-Your-Zipper-Up, I won't let you do this. I won't!"

Gypsy, the cat version of Lexi, met Molly at the door with her, *my-food-dish-is-empty,* look. And just to make sure her human understood she sat by it and bellowed, "Mrrrow."

"Sorry Gyps, you'll just have to wait." Molly threw

her purse on the couch. “Stan? Are you here?”

No answer. Good. He was probably at the B&B. She fished her cell phone from her purse, walked to the back porch. After stretching out on her deep-cushioned lounger, she called Avalee.

“Hello? MK?” Panic filled Avalee’s voice. “What’s wrong? Is Mom ok?”

“For heaven’s sakes, Ava. Can’t I call you just because?”

“Sorry. I just get nervous when there’s an ocean between us.”

“How are things in New Zealand?”

“Beautiful, but I’m ready to come home. Ty finished his photograph session yesterday. Now he starts the edits before sending them in. So, what’s up?”

“I’ll fill you in but first, when are you coming home?”

“Not sure, why?”

“Lexi needs us. Is there any way you can come home in a couple of days? I’m calling Jema to ask her the same thing.”

“Now you’re scaring me. What’s wrong?”

“Well, where do I start? Her ex, that sorry excuse for a man, has played the pity card and invaded her life—again.”

“Wait. What?”

“Oh, he says he’s dying, and I guess he is, otherwise he wouldn’t have been paroled a year early. But he has to stay under in-house arrest. The judge allowed a compassionate release, but someone had to take responsibility for him and seems that fell to Lex.”

Molly switched her phone to the other ear. “She needs us. I haven’t seen her this torn up since the last time that fool turned her world upside down."

"When do you need me?"

"Next Wednesday, for Wine and Whine. Think you can pull it off?"

"I will make it happen. I'll call Jema and fill her in. I'm sure she can pick me up in her private jet."

Molly Kate grinned. "It's so nice having rich friends."

"That it is. I'll let you know what Jema says."

"Oh, I hope it all works out. Won't Lexi be shocked?"

"We will make this work." Avalee paused. "We have to."

When Ava hung up, Molly Kate laid back her head and watched the fan blades furiously circle, creating enough breeze to make a small dent in the humidity. She smiled as she thought about Lexi's shock when Avalee and Jema walked into the room. Jema had lived in Italy for almost two years. They planned on returning to Moonlight by now but decided to stay a while longer. Molly didn't blame them, but on the other hand, she couldn't have stayed away so long. Even with humidity that weighed on your shoulders like a wet blanket, she loved her home.

Just when she got dozy, the phone rang. Avalee already? She checked. It was Stan. "Hello?"

"Hi, baby. Hey, are you going to the shop today?"

"I hadn't planned on it, why?"

"We need an assortment of muffins. I just rented a room here at the B & B for a local realtors meeting. They are meeting with Mayor Campbell to brainstorm."

"Will Lela Blodgett be there?" Molly Kate never liked the woman. From the first day of Stan's returning to Moonlight, Lela set her cap for him, winking at him with her Cleopatra-lined eyes. Someone needed to tell that hussy that a miniskirt and a social-security card didn't belong on the same woman.

"I'm afraid so."

"Hmph. She wouldn't happen to be allergic to nuts, would she? I have some lovely banana pecan muffins…"

"Remind me to stay on your good side." Just bring an assortment just in case someone really is allergic to nuts."

"Okay. I'll have them over in a jiffy."

"Thanks, baby, love you."

"Love you back." Molly rose and stretched. Life had smiled on her when it brought her Stan. Now, if only life would smile on Lexi.

Chapter Five

Purpose has many faces.

Memories flooded Toby's mind as he walked the two blocks to Cladie Mae's. He loved the homes along Washington Avenue. The two-story framed houses with tall windows, double doors, and wrap-around porches were at least ninety years or even older. The sprawling oaks were twice as old, and oh, what stories they could tell.

When he and Lexi purchased their home, it was, well, tired. But the old Victorian was a bargain. All the houses on the street were being sold because families migrated to the newer developments on the outskirts of town. With him in medical school and Lexi working her rear off, purchasing that house at an insanely low price had been a good move. Years of loving improvement on their investment had taken its value from thirty grand to over three hundred thousand. In fact, because young couples had purchased the houses on Washington Avenue, and restored them, the area was once again in high demand.

Just thinking about how hard Lexi had worked restoring their house added to the already unbearable burden he carried. He sure hoped Miss Cladie's homespun wisdom would help him lay some of that load down.

He smiled when he saw Miss Cladie's yard. There was no way to miss her house. It was the Disneyland of Washington Avenue. Every piece of yard art, every flowering bush, every bulbed flower, every birdbath, bird, and hummingbird feeder, evidenced her fun, nature-loving spirit. Ceramic squirrels chased each other on her white oak tree. And who could miss that ugly three-foot-high plywood cardinal that her friend, Felix, made for her? Nothing had changed since he left.

Miss Cladie stood from the swing where she sat on her screened-in porch. "Well, if it isn't Toby Lowe." She opened the door wide. "Get yourself in here and give me a hug."

Her words poured over his grimy soul like pure mountain water. The fragile façade of confidence he had erected began to waver, but he stiffened his resolve to appear like he had it all together.

"How about a cup of coffee? And I just took an apple pie out of the oven."

"Oh, Miss Cladie. I've walked straight out of hell into heaven."

She took his hand. "Come on in then. Let's have a nice chat."

He followed her into the kitchen and sat at the small drop-leaf table against a wall decorated with small Plaster of Paris fruits and vegetables she had made one winter long before he had married Lexi.

"Here you are." She set a warm slice of apple cinnamon pie topped with a thin slice of sharp cheddar in front of him.

"Thank you, Miss Cladie. This looks good. Real good."

"As I recall, you like coffee with cream. No sugar."

She placed a hot mug alongside his pie.

"Wow, great memory." He took a bite and turned his gaze to the ceiling as he savored the tender apple slices, the spicy burst of cinnamon, and the flaky crust. The sharp cheddar perfectly tempered the sweetness of the filling. "Ahhh, Miss Cladie. Will you marry me?"

"Not today, sugar. I'm too busy in my garden."

"Isn't it time to put the garden to bed?"

"Lord no, honey. I still have butter beans to pick. I've planted turnips, mustard and collard greens, and beets."

"I know I shouldn't be asking a lady this question, but, how old are you?"

"I'll be the big 8-0 my next birthday. Why do you ask?"

"You're so active."

Miss Cladie's expression crinkled with impish delight. "Sugar, I'm not D.O.A., just O-L-D."

Toby laughed. "Well, you're a hard worker for sure. In all my days of medical practice it was rare to find someone your age in such great shape." He ate the last bite of pie and finished his coffee. Then he pushed his dishes back and folded his arms on the table. "Miss Cladie. I need some advice."

Her expression deepened into maternal concern. "I'll do what I can."

"Well, you know the whole sordid story of my life."

Cladie nodded her head but said nothing. For this, he was thankful. He sighed, searching for what he wanted to say. But truth was, he just wanted someone to affirm him. Hadn't he learned a hard lesson? He'd paid his debt to society, he'd lost Lexi, his home, and his hope for a future. God. Wasn't that enough? His eyes burned as he studied Miss Cladie's gentle expression through blurred vision. His throat constricted and the tears he so valiantly held back now ran down his face.

"Toby, honey, tell me what is bothering you."

Her soft pat on his arm gave release to his years of sorrow and regret. He laid his face on his arms and cried until it seemed all the strength had drained out of his body.

He felt a tissue being pushed into his hand and looked up. "Thanks, Miss Cladie." After blowing his nose, he took in a deep breath.

"How about some nice cold sweet tea? And we can have this talk on the porch. There's something about nature that quiets our souls."

"Okay," He sucked in another deep breath and blew it out. "Sounds good."

She filled two bright-colored aluminum tumblers, handing him the electric blue one and keeping the candy-apple red one for herself. He followed her and sat in a rocker.

"Here." She passed him a washpan of speckled butterbeans she had picked before sunrise that morning. "Shell these."

He did as he was told. For a long time, they just sat, rocking, and shelling the beans. A funny little thrill rose inside every time he spied a creamy white bean with purple splotches.

After a while, Miss Cladie broke the silence. "Toby, honey, What got into you, anyway? Were you unhappy with Lexi? Had y'all grown apart?"

He rocked and kept shelling, keeping his eyes on the beans. "Miss Cladie, believe me, I've given this a lot of thought seeing how I had nothing else to do in prison, except work." He threw a handful of hulls in the wastebasket beside him. "I wasn't unhappy with Lex and I wouldn't say we had grown apart, but we were, well…stagnant. Stuck in a routine. I was trying to climb the ladder to hospital administrator." He glanced up at Miss Cladie. "Poor Lex. She turned herself inside out to help me up that ladder. There was never any time for just us and for that, I take full responsibility. Too bad I didn't realize it at the time."

"But why another woman? Or should I say, girl?"

Toby cringed. If anyone else had said that he would feel condemned—again. But there was no guile in Miss Cladie's statement.

"In my pathetic defense, there was nothing about the way she looked or acted that even hinted at high school. She represented herself as every bit college age. Her name is Claire. She came from an affluent family and was spending the weekend with her sister—who really was in college. It was Careers Day and Claire attended with her sister." He resumed shelling. "You know, now that I look back, Claire started pursuing me from the very beginning. Only, at the time I thought she was just real interested in studying medicine. After a short conversation about careers in medicine she asked me if she could take me to lunch on campus and talk some more." Toby looked out over the yard and shook his head. "I have to admit, she was attractive, and I liked the idea of spending more time with her."

"How on earth did it progress to a sexual relationship?"

"She emailed me." Toby handed Miss Cladie the bowl of shelled beans. "And she sent…pictures."

Miss Cladie's eyebrows domed above her glasses.

"It didn't take long for me to allow my imagination to run to the dark side. And it made me feel young, virile, desirable, instead of being what I truly was, a man on the south end of his fifties. Claire flirted and my ego lapped it up. And when that pretty, young thing invited me to an Ole Miss football game in Oxford, I accepted. I lied and told Lex that I was going with some of the docs from the hospital. I was pretty stoked about going to the game, but when we met, she said she had something to show me. It was a hotel room. And that is where all our games were held."

"Did you ever think of your wife?"

"Always on the way there and on the way home. The guilt was crushing, but not enough for me to turn away from Claire. In fact, the guilt made me distance myself from Lexi. All I could think of was my trysts in Oxford. It was like I was addicted."

"How long did this go on?"

"Only a couple of months. Then she drops the bomb on me that she is pregnant and I'm the father. At first, I didn't believe her. The reason is, just before Lexi and I married I had a medical issue. After some tests, the doc said more than likely I would never father children. He said it would be a miracle."

"Lordy, Toby. Did Lexi know that? She used to dream of being a mother."

Shame once again burned in his soul. "I know. No, I never told her. I was afraid she'd feel differently about me. So when she talked about trying for one, I kept putting her off saying it wasn't the right time. I guess I was hoping for that miracle. And then it looked like it came…but with the wrong woman."

"How did you find out about the pregnancy?"

"She emailed me. It was Lexi's and my anniversary. I had to come clean, so I told Lex everything." The events of that night played in his mind. "We both drank a glass of really expensive wine. Then I refilled our glasses, took her hand, and confessed. Naturally she was furious, and I got a face full of that expensive wine. But then an eerie calm came over her and she said she had to think, promising we would talk over what needed to be done about it the next day. I thought that meant that we could work it out. I didn't realize the calm was just the eye of the hurricane.

"The next morning, I tried to talk to Lex, but she said we would talk after we both got home from work. I can't tell you the relief I felt. I made promises all day to myself that I'd make it up to her, I'd take her on that trip to Europe that I'd been promising the past decade. But when I got home, all my stuff was in the yard and the locks had been changed."

Cladie nodded. "I remember."

"Then I got another email from Claire." The memory of that afternoon would haunt him forever. "She asked me to meet her at a local cafe. When I got there, her parents met me at the door and pushed me out onto the lot. Then her father signaled to a cop who was also waiting. I was dumbfounded and I asked what was going on. It was only then I found out she wasn't a junior in college, but in high school.

"I stared at Claire, but she couldn't face me. Her father demanded to know if it was true. If I had been having sex with his daughter. At first, I thought about lying, but if she was pregnant with my child, I couldn't lie and get away with it, so I told the truth. Right there I was arrested for statutory rape."

"Lord have mercy. What a mess. What happened with the child?"

"She was adopted. Claire wanted to keep her and told her parents to make me pay child support. But, as I said, they were not about to have their reputation sullied, so they forced her to give the child up."

"That was the best thing for the baby." Miss Cladie stood. "More tea?"

"Yes, ma'am. Please."

When she went inside, Toby mentally replayed Claire's visit while he was in prison. She'd gotten religion and came to confess about her deception and about the baby. She told him the baby had been her boyfriend's. They wanted to keep her, but the boy and his family were dirt poor and from the wrong side of town, so to speak. She knew her parents would never have approved of him and also knew he couldn't support a family. But when she met Toby, she contrived a plan that might allow her to keep the baby and maybe even marry her boyfriend. She decided to seduce him and tell her parents the baby belonged to a rich doctor. He, of course, would have to pay child support. And at the time she didn't see anything wrong with her plan. After all, a doctor could certainly afford it. Only she didn't consider what it would do to his marriage. However, her plan didn't work. She had to give up the child. To top it all off, her so-called boyfriend started dating another girl before his and Claire's baby was born.

Over time, the guilt weighed more and more on her until her new-found faith guided her in what to do.

Confess and ask for forgiveness.

Of course, he forgave her. After all, hadn't he been guilty of the same thing?

****

Toby sat back in the chair, closed his eyes, and rocked. It felt good relaxing in a nonjudgmental atmosphere. The fan above thinned the humidity and drew in the fragrance of nearby gardenia flowers. He glanced up to see a hummingbird hover by a feeder, taking a few sips before another chased it away.

The screen door squeaked, and Miss Cladie backed in with tea and sandwiches. "I know it is early for lunch, but we've got to fatten you up."

Toby sat up. "I'm game. Thanks, Cladie Mae." The beefy sandwich had a thick slice of meatloaf, mayo, and purple onion. His stomach growled. "Man, this looks good."

"Last night's supper. With Avalee and Ty gone to New Zealand, my grandson, Glen, comes over here several times a week and boy, can that child eat."

"Ava has a child?"

"He's Ty's boy. He has a daughter too, Skye. But they're mine all the same."

Toby took a big bite of the hearty sandwich and was delighted by the sweet, tangy glaze. "Man, Miss Cladie. This is fantastic." He took another bite.

"Why, thank you, hon." Miss Cladie looked as if each bite he took was a compliment. "I don't imagine they fed you too good in the penitentiary."

"No ma'am. After a while, I just lost my appetite. Ate enough to live, but there was no pleasure in it."

"Toby, I know a repentant man when I see one. You, son, are truly penitent. Tell me, what will it take to bring life back into your soul?"

He didn't have to think about his answer. "For Lexi to forgive me. But I'm afraid that'll never happen. I took so much from her. I can't even forgive myself."

Miss Cladie slapped her hand on her leg. "That's the first thing you must do."

"What's that?"

"Forgive yourself. You messed up. You made a horrible decision. Now admit it and move on. You served your time. It's over and done with." Miss Cladie stopped rocking and leaned forward, spearing the air with her finger. "You can't unscramble eggs, but that doesn't mean you can't do something wonderful with them."

"How do you mean?"

"The other day my neighbor's daughter, Junie, tore some leaves off my maple tree and let them fall to the ground. Now, those leaves were meant to remain on the tree and feed it. But because of decision made by Junie, they were stripped from their purpose…or were they?"

Now Toby leaned forward. "I'm listening."

"Next time I mow I'll grind those leaves up and leave them to compost back into the soil, where they will still feed the tree, only in a different way." She rose, stepped over to Toby and took his hands. "Shug, you still have purpose. You're still a healer. Only now in a different way. Talk to men, talk to young people, let them know about the consequences on their future by bad decisions." She squeezed his hands. "But like I said, first, you are going to have to forgive yourself and make a new decision to move forward. Use this awful experience for the good of others."

Again, tears filled his eyes. Yes, he was a broken

man. Yes, he had suffered the consequences and learned the lesson. But how to move forward?

As if reading his mind Miss Cladie said, "Come with me to church Sunday. I'll introduce you to Pastor Dixon. Tell him your story. He'll be a compassionate guide and friend."

"Thank you, Miss Cladie. I'd like that."

"Be here at eight. I'll feed you breakfast, and we can walk to church."

Toby smiled. "Miss Cladie, if your breakfast is anything like that sandwich, I'll need to walk."

She gave him a hug. "Tell Lexi I want her to come to the house for coffee soon."

"Will do." He hugged the tiny woman and laid his head on top of her wavy, blue-white hair. "And thanks."

She reached in her pocket and pushed something in his hand. "Here. Go get you something that fits."

He looked at the two folded hundred-dollar bills. "Oh, no ma'am, I can't."

She crossed her arms over her chest. 'Now don't you back-talk me, Toby Lowe. Get yourself to town." She smiled and walked back into the house.

On the way back to Lexi's, Toby thought about what Miss Cladie had said. Before he reached her yard, he knew just what he would do. He hoped and prayed it would help Lexi, too. To strengthen his resolve, he picked up a maple leaf as a reminder, and walked up the porch steps.

****

Toby walked inside and put the leaf on the dinette table. After his talk with Miss Cladie, he wanted his life to count for something. But first things first. He walked to the patio and lifted his gaze through the large oak's leafy branches, focusing on the blue sky peeking between the thick leaves.

"God, I know I've asked for your forgiveness. More than once. But now, I'm asking you to help me forgive myself and to show me what to do with the scrambled eggs of my life."

His throat tightened and he waited for the wave of emotion to ease. "Whatever you want me to do with what's left of my life here, please make it clear. And God? Help me make things up to Lex. Show me a way to get through to her."

He stood waiting for some kind of sign. Light breaking through the branches, a cloud of butterflies. But nothing happened. Still, he felt peace and that was something he hadn't felt in years.

Back in the house he thought about his promise to go to church with Miss Cladie. He only had two pairs of pants and two shirts. All were too large for him. He studied his reflection in the mirror. He could use a haircut, too. Time and prison had not been kind. There was no place to go from here but up. He grabbed his wallet and fished in his pocket for the money Miss Cladie had given him. He had money left over from his prison wages, so all combined should allow him to buy something that fit and get his hair trimmed.

The walk to town was only a few blocks, but he decided to call for an Uber instead. His lung capacity was still pretty good, but it wasn't worth the risk. He needed all the time and breath he could get.

Chapter Six

Dreamers

I hated going to my meeting with Sid while in a bad mood. Of course, he'd seen and endured all my many moods. He was the most patient man I'd ever known. He had to be. I mean, I'm not even in the same ballpark as his ex-wife and he endured her for years. What kind of woman would just up and leave her two boys? They were only fourteen and sixteen, for heaven's sake. And then what does she do? After all those years off the radar she just shows up at her mother's house saying that the guy she'd been living with had kicked her out. By now their son Chris was married and had a child. Cody was in his second year of college. Neither wanted anything to do with Barbara. But at their grandmother's urging they came over for Christmas like they did every year, only this time they didn't stay for dinner. Chris didn't even bring his family to meet his mother.

Barbara was outraged by this slight. But it didn't faze the boys. Chris calmly told her exactly where she could spend eternity…and it wasn't Heaven.

After they left their grandmother's they went to Miss Cladie's for Christmas leftovers and told Sid what happened. That patient man just shook his head. In my humble opinion, he dodged a bullet.

I stopped at Molly Kate's biz for coffee and lemon scones. This combination always elevated my spirits. Scones and a happy Lexi was doubly good for poor Sid.

When I walked into his office, I called in my most cheery voice, "Good morning! I come bearing gifts."

"Ahh, my telepathy worked. Coffee and cinnamon scones?"

"Lemon."

He smiled, peering over his glasses. "I need to work on my mental powers. But lemon sounds great."

"I might or might not have heard *cinnamon*, but I like lemon." I smiled and handed him a coffee and scone. His white hair lay in soft waves and his smile created small crinkles around his ocean-blue eyes. He had what I'd call a laid-back charisma that resonated with the voters when he ran for mayor. Especially the female voters, young and old alike.

"Um, Lex? Everything okay?"

I snapped out of my thoughts. Quickly recovering and trying to save some dignity, I blurted, "Oh, sorry. My mind was somewhere else."

"Let me guess. Toby?"

Um, no, but… "Yeah, it's awkward."

"Wanna talk about it?"

"Nope. I want to talk about my idea about the old hosiery factory. Do you know who owns it?"

"The city had to take it over, but there are no plans for it."

"Well, in my opinion that place is an eyesore. It's the first thing people see when they drive into the city limits and that's a terrible foreboding about Moonlight as a tourist spot. So, I have an idea and I hope you like it."

Sid took a bite of his scone and said, "Shoot."

"I want to turn it into an event space that would draw small to medium conferences."

"I like it." He inclined his head, momentarily lost in thought, then said, "And it should have a modern industrial vibe."

"Yes. And we will have state-of-the-art technology."

He set his half-eaten scone on the table. "That large office area on the top floor would be great for that. Plenty of space for meetings." He picked up his coffee cup and paced the room, gesticulating with his arms. "And we could make a rooftop garden area and set up a bar for evening happy hour and networking." He slapped the table. "I love it Lexi. Let's do this. Of course, we will have to run it by the town council."

"We can handle them." I bit into my scone and savored it. For the first time in weeks, I felt like myself. Creating with Sid had given me oxygen and it felt good.

****

Sid looked forward to his meetings with Lexi. She was always so vivacious and such a smartass, but in a good way. A funny way. But lately she'd not been herself. He could tell she tried to cover her low spirits, but he'd known her a long time and he hadn't seen her like this since finding out about Toby's affair with that teenager.

What a shocker. The guy was on his way to the top and it was often on Lexi's shoulders where he stood to get onto the next rung. She did everything for him. Sid supposed that was why his dalliance was such a bewilderment..

"See, Sid?" Lexi turned her computer screen for

him to see. "This is the place where I got my idea for making over the hosiery factory into an event space. This article says this place in Northwest Arkansas is pretty popular."

"Print it out for me. I'd like to read up on it."

Sid had to admire her. She was a little spitfire. With her on his team, he couldn't help but be successful. And she was beautiful. That Nathan guy obviously noticed too, but something about him bothered Sid. He knew he shouldn't make snap judgements on someone he'd never met. After all, he might be a stand-up guy. Sid sure hoped so. Lexi had been burned—bad—and he didn't want to see that happen again.

Lexi's voice broke into his thoughts. "Hey, is there a way we could take a look inside?"

"Sure. Since the city took it over, I have the keys."

Lexi looked up and smiled. "Great. I'll grab my sketch pad."

Sid sorted through his desk drawer and found the keys.

"Got the pad." Lexi held it up. "Now, let's go dream together."

That sounded nice. Dreaming together. He'd always been a dreamer, but no one ever appreciated that part of his personality, that is, until Lexi.

****

Creating. Just the thing to get my mind off my life. While Sid unlocked the door, I looked around the outside of the building. It was almost a perfect square sitting on the corner of the block. The windows on each floor were arched with intricate brick work over each arch. The old brick was mottled red and brown with some missing in places. Across the front was a faded sign painted on the building that read, *Moonlight Hosiery Factory.* We would keep that for history's sake.

One idea chased another in my mind until I noticed an abandoned warehouse next door.

"Sid!"

He turned, startled, "What?"

"Another idea. We need overnight space for the attendees, right?"

"Go on."

"Well, the problem is that there isn't any place for attendees to stay except for the B&B or the hotels along the freeway." I pointed to the building next to the factory. "That warehouse would make a perfect boutique hotel. Does it belong to the city?"

"It does, but…"

"Now hear me out. We could continue with the industrial look on the first-floor lobby and breakfast room. Then have ensuite rooms on the second and third floors. Oh, and also on the first floor we could have rooms for handicap access."

"I don't know Lex. That would be a pretty expensive project."

"But just think of the businesses it would bring. And remember, Avalee and I have a lot of contacts. We could bring national attention to Moonlight, only if we have a space to offer tourists on that scale."

Sid looked at me with that cute, crooked grin and shook his head. "You make it hard to argue. But it will have to be approved by the town council. Are you ready to do battle? We are asking them to let us not only take on the hosiery factory but the warehouse too. This is a big—no—an *astronomical* project."

I had to admit to myself that it would be more like a miracle, but I showed more confidence than I felt. "Oh, I think I can throw some hands if I need to."

"All right then. I'll call up the city architectural department to draw up some sketches. Then we can go into battle."

A thought occurred to me. "No, call Audy. He's the best architect in the south."

"Audy it is, then."

"Also, ask him to give us an idea about how many rooms we can fit in the hotel." I wrapped my arms around Sid's neck and hugged him. "This is going to be so great. I'm so excited."

A white curl fell over his forehead. He raised his eyebrows and grinned. "I'd say you are."

What was I doing? I pulled away. "Sorry, I guess the southern woman in me got a little touchy-feely."

He leaned forward. "I don't mind."

To be honest, neither did I. The urge to go up on my tip toes and kiss him felt tempting. Thankfully my phone rang. I held up my finger. "Just a sec. I need to get this."

Sid nodded and walked off to have another look around.

"Hey, Molly Kate. What's up?"

"Hey, girl. Listen, can you stop by the shop? We need to set a date for Whine Wednesday, so I can tell Avalee and Jema."

"Sure, I'll be by in a bit."

"Okay, see ya, shug."

When I hung up, Sid turned around. "So, we've got our battle plan?"

"I think so."

He swept his hand in front of him and bowed. "On to battle then, fair lady."

I curtsied. "As you wish, my lord."

When we left, I wasn't thinking of battles, but of a certain white-haired knight."

****

Sid pushed his hands deep in his pockets and scuffed along the walk to his office. He couldn't get Lexi out of his mind. She'd always been a kick in the butt, get with the program, kind of person. He needed that kind of friend in his life. Sure, he was full of ideas, but seeing them through had always been hard for him. Not Lexi. She became the energy behind his ideas. No wonder Toby was a success. And then for him to throw it all away. What was that man thinking? Why would anyone cheat on her? If she were his, he'd…

That thought pulled him back and he realized a shift had taken place in him. Lexi was becoming more than a collaborator to him. Not a good thing. Besides, who was he when compared to *the* Nathan Wolfe? Who was anyone when compared to him?

Toby came to mind again. It had to be hard to be back in what was once his home, with who was at one time his wife, and who is now dating a celebrity. Did Toby have any friends? All those years of glad-handing to build his reputation and career probably didn't make for any kind of real relationship.

Poor guy. Sid couldn't help it. He always had a soft spot for down and outers. Lexi said she was meeting with Molly Kate. Maybe it was a good time to drop by and see Toby. Yeah, that's what he'd do. Maybe take him to lunch.

****

When Sid pulled onto the driveway, Toby came to the door and pushed it open. He got out of his car and walked toward the porch.

"Hi ,Toby, long time, no see."

A smile of recognition revealed the old Toby. "Sid?"

"The very one." He walked up the steps. "How are you?"

"Been better." Toby gestured for Sid to come in. "Lexi's gone, so it's safe to be in *her* part of the house."

"Yeah, I just left her. She has big plans for the old hosiery factory and warehouse."

"That's our girl. Full of ideas." Toby eased onto a kitchen chair and indicated for Sid to do the same. "Coffee?"

"Sure. Thanks."

Toby stood and walked to the coffee maker. "Sugar? Cream?

"Black."

Sid covertly watched him and tried to see the man he once knew. The once tall and proud Dr. Lowe was now gaunt and broken. He had served time for his bad choice and it showed.

"Here you go." Toby set the cup on the table and then returned to his chair and took a sip from his. "Man, I never realized how much I missed good coffee."

Sid nodded, at a loss. What do you say to a man who has been locked away for so long?

Toby smiled. "Kind of awkward, isn't it?"

Embarrassed, Sid could only smile and nod. "You could say that. I mean, 'hey, how have you been' just seems wrong."

Toby chuckled. "Yeah, those *meet on the street* platitudes don't work in this case."

"Really, how are you now?" Sid genuinely wanted to know.

"I figured Lexi would have filled you in."

"No, we mainly talk about reimagining Moonlight."

"Did you know I'm terminally ill?"

The shock of this statement sank deep to his core. "No."

"Lung cancer. I'm not sure how much time I have. I could fight it with treatment, but the prognosis is still terminal. I feel pretty good now and would like to stay that way and savor life while I still can."

This explained the gauntness. Compassion replaced any kind of judgement Sid may have felt. "Hey, want to go to lunch? It's on me."

"I'd like that. I was just about to schedule an Uber to go into town."

"You have business in town?"

"I need some clothes. I've lost a lot of weight. Prison food will do that for you. And I need a haircut for the few hairs I have left." He winced. "You've kept your mop."

"Yeah, thanks to my granddad's genes. So, let's go to lunch and when you are finished in town give me a call and I'll take you home."

"Hey, man, that'd be great. Thanks."

"Anything for a friend."

Sid noticed his statement took Toby by surprise. Toby looked down and briefly pinched his nose. It had probably been a long time since anyone had considered him a friend.

Toby glanced up. “Thanks, I really appreciate it.”

Sid thought about Lexi and how having Toby back in her life was so hard on her. But he also knew this could possibly be the best thing that could have happened for both of them. One needing forgiveness and one needing to forgive.

Life worked in mischievous ways.

Chapter Seven

The lesson of the maple leaf

When I walked into—more like *pushed into*—the crowd in Molly Kate's shop, she looked up from the counter and waved. How on earth did she spot me wedged between taller bodies or hear the jingle on the door over the din? She motioned for me to follow her, so I excused and pardoned myself all the way to the counter. MK squeezed between customers and met me.

"I need a bigger space." Molly Kate blew a strand of hair from her forehead and led the way to a table she'd reserved for us.

"Amen to that." We passed a display of interesting looking muffins. "You need a sampler for those?"

"Absolutely, girlfriend."

"Well, I might oblige you if you'll also throw in a latte."

Molly Kate called—more like yelled, "Cherrell, two lattes. Full fat. And muffins. Bring that jelly I made to go with them too."

"Yes, ma'am, I'll be there directly." Cherrell's tone of voice said something quite different, suggestive of exactly what MK could kiss. Lexi had to smile.

"Okay, let's talk about Whine Wednesday. Zooming Ava and Jema is out. I checked and Avalee is in New Zealand. It's already tomorrow morning there.

And Italy is seven hours ahead, so we'd have to meet during office hours and that's no fun. All that said, it looks like it is just me and you."

I tried to not let my crushing disappointment show.

Cherrell stumbled over with the lattes, muffins, and jelly. "Here you go."

Molly Kate smiled. "Thanks, Lady Bug." She turned to me. "Ain't she the sweetest thing?"

This did little to mollify *Lady Bug.* Cherrell crossed her arms. "Anything else before I go back to *work*?"

Molly dismissed her frazzled granddaughter with a flutter of her fingers. "No darling, that's all for now."

Cherrell raised her gaze to the ceiling, turned around, and trudged away.

"That girl's gonna quit on you."

"No she's not." MK took a sip of her latte. "Mmm, just like I taught her to make it. Anyway, she knows this will one day be half hers if she wants it. She's just a little stressed 'cos it's a busy day."

I picked up the warm muffin. "Flavor? Please say they are your Pumpkin Spice. I mean, it is almost fall."

"But not quite yet. I'm trying out a new savory. These are bacon and pepper jack cheese."

"But I want sweet." I sounded like a four-year-old."

"See that jar of red pepper jelly? It will cure your sweet tooth. Come on. Give it a try."

"Ookaay." I dipped my knife in the pepper jelly and spread it on my muffin, then took a bite. "Hey. This is *good*."

"I know, right?" Molly Kate bobbed her head.

The star of the show was that smoked bacon, but

the cheese made the muffin so rich. And then that little after burn at the end from the sweet pepper jelly made it sing. What could I say? "MK, you've done it again!"

"Thanks, hon. I know." Molly grinned as she spread jelly on hers. "So how was your meeting with Sid?"

"Great!" I faltered wondering if I should mention my new idea for a hotel. "Umm, there *is* one little thing and I hope you won't be angry with me." I suddenly lost my nerve and studied my muffin like it had the answer to curing cancer.

"For heaven's sakes. What on God's green earth are you talking about?"

Ok, might as well take the dive. "I have this idea, about, well, about turning the old warehouse into a hotel."

Molly Kate tilted her head and stared at me with her feline eyes. I felt like a mouse about to be pounced on. "The warehouse?"

"Yeah, because we are turning the old hosiery factory into an event space. So, in order to attract small to medium conferences they need some place in town to stay and not have to go out on Hwy 22 to find a chain hotel." I lifted my hand and continued. "I know we have your place but there are only eight rooms."

"Oh, I'm not worried about business. In fact, that will probably attract business for us year around. But the warehouse? How on earth?"

"Audy can work miracles. Sid's probably with him now discussing plans as we speak."

"He needs to be a miracle worker for that old place."

"He's just the man for the job." I pressed my finger

into the crumbs and stuck them in my mouth. "Something else happened while we were looking at it."

"Oh?"

"Yeah, it was the weirdest thing."

Molly Kate's eyebrows shot up. "What?"

I knew that'd get her full attention. "I kinda got caught up in the moment and I hugged Sid. I mean *really* hugged him. Body to body.

A slow smile spread across her face. "And?"

"It was like a slow burn, not electricity, but a steady, growing burn."

She clasped her hands under her chin and said in her highest voice, "Exciting."

I put my hands up. "Whoa, wait. I'm with Nate. Remember? We have a good thing going here. Just the way I like it."

"Are you and Nate exclusive?"

I thought a moment. "I think so. I mean, we don't see each other a lot, but we do talk every week."

"But honey, face it. Unless he is willing to live here or you live in New York City, I can't see how it could ever develop into something, well, you know, permanent." She put her hand on mine. "You aren't getting any younger. You need a soulmate. Could you call Nate a soulmate?"

"I'm not sure."

"Well, we can talk more about it on Wednesday. Your place or mine?"

"Let's make it my place. That way we won't have your guests knocking on the door wanting something."

"Okay, your place. How about six-thirty?"

"That'll be fine." I stood and took my purse off the

back of the chair. "I'm sure going to miss Avalee and Jema. It's just not the same with them gone."

"I know. I'll miss them too." She hugged my shoulder. "But we've got each other, so let's just think on that."

I squeezed her hand. "Love you, girl."

"Love you back." I turned to leave, but then stopped and faced her. "Bring orange rolls. I think that'll soothe over my bad mood."

"Will do, honey bunch."

The thought of orange rolls mollified me, kinda. Now to warn Toby about Whine Wednesday and his need to disappear.

I walked into my house and threw my keys on the table. "Toby?"

No answer. The door to his room was open so I peeked inside. Nope. Not there. I walked through to the patio to see if he was there. Not there either. One thing I did notice was that his room looked like the Moonlight Maids had cleaned it. A far cry from when I was married to the slob.

Where was he? Then a thought burned through my brain. He had better not be snooping in my room. I high tailed it across the house and ran into my room. No one.

Weird. I wandered back to the kitchen and noticed a note on the kitchen bar.

Lexi, gone to lunch with Sid. Then shopping. Sid will drive me home a little later. Toby

Gone to lunch with…Sid? *Sid? What?*

I wadded the note up and tossed it in the trash. What was Sid up to? He's supposed to be *my* friend. He'd better not go to the dark side. We certainly couldn't work together if that happened. My mood grew even more gloomy—if that was even possible. Wednesday couldn't come fast enough.

Two hours later I heard a car door slam. I looked out the living room window to see Sid pulling off the driveway and Toby, with several shopping bags in tow, walking to the porch. I eased back from the window and hurried to my room. I just couldn't deal with him now. I decided to take a long hot bath. When I finished and dressed, I decided to kill more time and straighten my dresser. While I pulled out drawers and refolded underwear and matched socks a tiny voice from somewhere in my head asked, *why are you hiding in your bedroom?*

I was being ridiculous. I slammed the drawer shut and mentally gave myself a good talking to. *Lexi Lowe, you are in YOUR house. Quit acting like an idiot.* I took a deep breath, walked down the hall to the living room, through the dining room, and into the kitchen. Toby stood at the stove cooking something that smelled, well, delicious. My mouth watered, reminding me that I hadn't eaten anything but a muffin all day.

He turned around and smiled. "I thought I'd make one of your favorites, steak and parmesan potatoes."

I stared at him. His hair was neat, and his clothes fit him. If I looked hard enough, I could almost see the college boy I fell in love with. Except for his receding hairline and the hollow look around his blue eyes, I saw him as he once was. Memories grabbed me by the throat and squeezed.

I stood there with my mouth hanging open like a baby waiting for her next bite of strained bananas. He poured me a glass of wine and motioned to the bar stool. "Have a seat. It'll be ready in a few minutes."

I took the wine and drank it in two gulps.

He put his hands out. "Hey, that's no way to drink wine." After refilling my glass, he gave a sly smile. "And if you are tempted to throw it in my face," he held up a cheap bargain brand, "use this."

I couldn't help it. I smiled back, remembering back when I doused him in my anger, years ago. "So, what's up with Sid? How did you two wind up going to lunch?"

He shrugged. "I don't really know. I was about to get an Uber into town because I needed a haircut and get some clothes that fit. But then Sid drove up, we talked a while and then he offered to drive me to town and buy me lunch. We talked over old times." He took the cast iron pan out of the stove and laid the steaks on a plate to rest. After topping each with a pat of butter he glanced up at me. "It is nice to have a friend. I never realized that before now."

I tried to harden my heart, but it was getting more difficult. Besides, I just finished my second glass of wine and my stomach was growling like a momma bear protecting her cubs.

Dinner was delicious. Conversation came easier than usual. As I expected, Toby hinted about my relationship with Nate, and then Sid. He was fishing for information.

Fish away, Toby boy. I'm not telling you a darned thing.

As politely as I could I told him my relationships were really none of his business. To my surprise, he nodded, stood, and stacked the dishes.

"Thanks for supper." I yawned and waved my hand toward the sink. "Leave the dishes, I'll do them tomorrow."

"I'll clean up, no worries." He turned and looked at me over his shoulder. "Night."

"Night." I dragged my rear to my room and wondered, *who is this man?*

****

By Wednesday, I'd managed to come up with my whine list. But it seemed kinda petty, even to me. Toby was in my home using my utilities, occupying my den—which, by the way, is where my one and only fireplace is located—and I had to be dressed to walk around the house. Compared with the folks living in the homeless tent city outside of town? Yep. Downright pitiful. But maybe the wine would help me think of more things to complain about.

Molly Kate came waltzing through my door promptly at six-thirty with orange rolls fresh from the oven. "Okay, the whining can begin. I'm here!"

I reached inside the basket where she toted the rolls. "I need this first."

She slapped my hand, "Get out of there."

"Nope." I grabbed one and trotted across to the living room.

Where her orange rolls were concerned, she might as well have tried to chop my hand off. I was gonna have me a roll.

She just shook her head and went to the kitchen while I enjoyed my love affair with the pastry. There is an art to eating them which comes with many steps. First, the visual. I examined the fat, fluffy, spiral covered with glaze. Second, pull off the first spiral. This is the crunch part and as yummy as it is, it's not my favorite. But the next spiral gets down to business.

The soft bun is infused with the tart marmalade. And then the crescendo of the orange roll orchestra—the tender center dripping with the tangy, buttery, glaze. I popped it in my mouth and savored that last bite that melted in my mouth. The perfect bite making all things in the world right. At least for that moment.

"Are you through yet?" Molly Kate stood in the hall with hands on hips. "For heaven's sake, I've never seen anyone so methodical about eating a roll."

I licked icing off each finger one at a time. "There is a right way and a wrong way to do everything."

"Well, come on in the kitchen and let's get the wine uncorked." While I washed my hands in the kitchen sink, MK pulled out the red and the white. "Where's Toby?"

"I sent him to Miss Cladie's. I didn't want him here sneaking around eavesdropping and saying the window was up or the door was cracked." Just as I wiped my hands on a dish towel the front door squeaked open.

My ears went on red alert. That had better not be Toby. Then a very familiar voice called, "Knock, knock."

I swung around to see Avalee and Jema walk into the kitchen.

"Oh my god!" My hands went to my mouth and tears blinded me as I ran into their open arms. There we were. Four friends sobbing in a group hug, back together as we always should have been.

"I can't believe y'all are really here." I glanced at MK. "You knew all along, didn't you?"

"Gotcha." Molly Kate grinned, then nodded toward the bar. "Ladies, let's pour our wine and drink up."

After a sip, I teared up again. "Gee, after this, I

can't think of a thing to whine about."

Molly Kate bumped me with her hip. "Oh, after a couple glasses, you'll get loosened up."

"Hush up, MK." But she was right.

Avalee giggled. "Nothing's changed." She glanced at Jema. "Eh, Jems?"

"Nothing." Jema put her arm around Lexi's shoulder and squeezed. "Thank goodness."

Our first glass went down really fast.

"I suggest we refill and get caught up before we start our whines." Molly Kate held up two bottles. "Red or White?"

When the refills were done, we gathered in the living room. I drank in the sight before me. It had been months since I'd seen Avalee and over a year since I'd seen Jema. "Y'all go first."

"Well," said Jema. "Levi and I are coming home soon."

We all jumped up and squealed. Wine sloshed precariously in our glasses.

"When?" I settled back on the couch.

"We are planning to return sometime next year."

"Are you selling the villa?" I sure hoped not. It would be nice having a place to stay in the rare case of me going back to Europe.

"No, we're keeping it and the staff."

Molly Kate grinned, nodding her head. "The staff. I like that. Wish I had staff."

I nudged MK. "You do. His name is Stan."

"Anyway," Jema smiled. "We are keeping the villa for friends and business associates who would like a place to stay while visiting Italy. And the staff will keep the house and grounds up. Besides, we couldn't leave them jobless."

"Where do you plan to live when you come back?" My mind went immediately to AJ and Junie.

"We've decided to build and hope it's okay to stay with you, MK, while the house is being built.

"That sounds good to me." Molly Kate leaned forward and stage whispered, "I'll give you a good price."

Jema put her hands up. "Oh no. We will pay full price, period."

"What about AJ and Junie?" I had to know.

Jema swiped the air with her hand. "Oh, we signed the house over to them a long time ago.

I always teared up at the memory of AJ's surprise and Junie's delight, as only a child could express, when Jema and Levi offered them a home. Every so often I play the *what if's* over and over in my mind. What if Levi, a filthy rich Canadian, hadn't disguised himself as a homeless man in order to find acceptance for who he really was and not for what he owned? He never would have met and befriended AJ in the tent city where the homeless camped on the outskirts of town. What if Jema had rejected Levi because he was poor, dirty, and so obviously different from the folks in Moonlight? She and Levi wouldn't have married, and her house wouldn't have been available for such a deserving man and his child.

But it did happen. It was nice to remember that sometimes things do work out for the best.

"Earth to Lexi." Molly sashayed to me and refilled my glass. "Time to begin."

"Oh, yeah. Okay, who first?" I certainly didn't want to start.

"Well, I'll start since I really don't have a lot to whine about." Jema teared up. "My whine is, I sure do miss you girls." She ran her fingers under her eyes. "I love Italy, and Levi is my soulmate and best friend, but there's just something about you girls. You are the breath and light to my soul. I feel as if I'm growing dim. And now, just in this past hour, I'm charged." Fresh tears trickled down Jema's face. "I can't wait to return to Moonlight." She grinned. "Betcha, you never thought you'd hear me say that."

Molly Kate piped up. "Nope, but I have to say, I'm glad you did." She turned and gave Avalee's knee a playful slap. "What's your whine?"

Ava looked at each of us, one at a time, directly in our eyes. She sighed. "There's going to be a baby next May."

A collective gasp sucked all the oxygen out of the room. No one moved. I could hear my heart in my ears. Ava stared at us for a hot second, then dropped her head and her shoulders began to shake. Poor thing. We all huddled around her. But she wasn't crying. Heck, I sure would be. She was laughing. LAUGHING. *What*?

"Gotcha." Now she was full-on howling, holding her stomach, rocking back and forth. None of us laughed. We just stared at her like a tree full of owls. When she finally got a hold of herself, she realized it really wasn't funny. She wiped her face, and then began to cry.

What the heck is going on?

"Did someone spike Avalee's wine? The girl has gone mad." I sat beside her and handed her a tissue. "What is it, Ava?"

She wiped away tears. "It's Skye. She and her

football hero, Duff."

Molly Kate sat back. "Oh lord."

"I know." Ava blew her nose. "Sorry about scaring ya'll, but when I said there was going to be a baby and the look on your faces, well, it was too funny." She looked at her lap and shook her head. "Ty is pretty upset. We both are, but I can't regret a child. He or she has as much right to be celebrated as any child does."

"What's she going to do?" I thought of Nate and his aspirations for her as a journalist.

"They are going to marry. They had planned on that anyway but wanted to wait until they graduated. If the baby waits until the due date, mid-May, she will get to walk. Duff will go on to get his masters in youth counseling."

"So the girl gets stuck at home with the child." Lexi slapped her leg. "Figures."

"No, she's going to continue with her writing. I talked to Nate and he's going to help her along." A wistful look crossed Avalee's expression. "I never had a baby, and I'll admit, I'm actually looking forward to this experience."

"There's nothing like it." Jema took Ava's hand. "You will be wrapped around that child's finger like a stripe on a candy cane."

"Ty will too, only he doesn't know it." Avalee frowned. "We haven't told his parents. With his mother so sick, I just don't think we should."

"Is she in hospice?" I never liked that old battle ax, especially because of her hatefulness toward Avalee. But since Ava and Ty's wedding she softened and now loves Ava like one of her own.

"No, she is staying in her home. Hospice comes to

her. And Momma goes over every day to sit with her. They talk and laugh over their old school days together. Mom reads to her sometimes." Another tear trickled down Avalee's cheek. "Ty will be home in a couple of days. We will spend all the time we can with her."

Avalee's whine made mine seem so…so selfish and mean-spirited. She stood, walked to the orange rolls, and put one on a plate. Returning to her chair she cut the thing *in half* with a knife.

I cringed. "That's *not* the proper way to eat an orange roll."

Avalee lifted her gaze to the ceiling and then back at me. "Here we go again. Lexi Lowe, you need to copyright the proper method of eating orange rolls."

"Don't think I won't." I crossed my arms over my chest and averted my eyes so I could not witness the orange roll impudence. Not quite ready to whine, I pointed to MK. "Your turn."

"I really don't have much to whine about."

"Oh, there has to be something."

Molly thought a minute. "Okay. The guests in my house refuse to follow the one safety rule I insist on and that is no smoking in the mansion. But it seems I always have one who hides out in the library and smokes a pipe."

Jema said, "So, you've decided it isn't Stan."

"I don't think so. Every time we hug or kiss, I sniff him like a hound dog on the trail and come up with nothing. No pipe smoke. No peppermint. If it is him, then he must change his clothes each time. I guess he might do that. But sakes alive, he could smoke at home. I wouldn't mind and I've told him that."

"Maybe the guests who smoke pipes bring

peppermint oil to hide the fact they've been smoking." Molly folded her leg under her. "We take such care with the fireplaces. It would be tragic for the old place to burn down because of a forgotten pipe or hot ash smoldering on the rug. Besides all that. Rules are rules."

The room grew quiet and then all eyes zeroed in on me. I swallowed and then took a deep breath.

"Okay. Here goes." I blew out a breath. "When I first got that letter from Toby, I complained about being a prisoner in my own house, not being able to use my fireplace…"

Avalee frowned. "But you never used it in the first place."

"I know, Ava. I know. That has been pointed out to me many times." I rolled my eyes. "But what I've come to realize is that because Toby stomped all over my heart, I don't know if I'll ever be able to trust it to another man. Does that mean I'm doomed to living alone the rest of my life?"

Jema pulled her knees up and rested her chin on them. "What about Nathan."

"I like him. I like him a lot. But I don't trust him. Not because of anything he's done. He's been great. But our long-distance relationship keeps us from exploring anything deeper." I swirled my Syrah. "Besides, I see him on television around some pretty sophisticated women."

Avalee nodded her head. "That's his tribe all right. But I know he really cares for you."

"Lex, what would it take for you to forgive Toby?" Jema peeled off the first spiral of her orange roll, bless her.

I thought about her question and I honestly didn't know. I'd treasured my hurt for so long that it was lodged in my soul like a splinter so deep a scar had formed over it. Sometimes I didn't know it was there and then other times it hurt like the dickens. Finally, I admitted, "I really don't know….revenge maybe?"

"Hmmph." Molly Kate lowered one eyebrow Elvis style. "I'd say prison is a good start on revenge."

"But I feel like if I forgive him, it is like saying what he did is okay."

"Sugar." Molly Kate's voice took on a rare gentle quality. "*Even he* doesn't say it was okay."

My mind flopped like a bass out of water. To be honest, I'd never thought about what it would take to forgive him.

Avalee chimed in. "Honey, it isn't fair what happened to you, and it wasn't okay. But that's in your past. Don't stay chained to it. You are only hurting yourself."

Jema walked over and sat beside me. "Avalee is right. You need the freedom to love again."

I closed my eyes and tilted my face to the ceiling, while sighing. "I don't know if I can."

Jema stood and pulled me to my feet and the girls circled around me. MK was the first to speak, "Of course you can. You are one of the strongest women I know."

Avalee spoke up. "I agree. And if you listen to truth instead of pain, you'll find your way to freedom."

"And that truth," said Jema, "is to reach forward to what lies ahead and close the door on the pain of your past."

I nodded. They were right. My forever-sister-friends had sparked a tiny flame in me. A candle in a cave. I vowed to protect that tiny flame and prayed it would steadily grow into a blaze.

Our Whine meeting ended early. Avalee and Jema were dead on their feet from jetlag and since Avalee was home for good and Jema was staying a few weeks, we didn't feel so bad about cutting the meeting short. Truth be known, I had a lot to digest anyway.

Once alone again, I decided a hot lavender soak sounded good. I'd just relax in the warm fragrance and let the evening replay itself in my mind. I locked the front door since Toby knew where I hid the key and filled the tub.

When I immersed in the hot water, I let my mind drift off into nothingness and relished the feeling of soft water and the herbaceous scent of the bath salts. When the water grew tepid, I stepped out of the tub and wrapped in one of my extra soft towels, then slathered on lotion.

I threw on my well-worn nighty and decided to go to bed and read. Something I hadn't indulged in since the letter. Even in my sheerest gown, I was still hot, either from the bath or from my constant internal summer, I wasn't sure. A glass of iced tea sounded good. On my way to the kitchen, I noticed a flickering light on the front porch. I hurried to the front window. Toby? On *my* front porch. In *my* space? Didn't he remember the rules?

Anger flared in me but then I remembered the earlier discussion. I needed to break this habit. The only person with their guts on fire was me. I took a deep breath and walked outside.

"Toby? What's going on."

He stood, eyes widening, and cleared his throat. I realized my gown wasn't covering much, so I crossed my arms over my breasts.

"I know this is your space, but I wanted to talk to you." He gestured to a pitcher on the side table. "I made shandies, just like you like them, British style."

On a warm, sultry night, the crisp beer and sparkling lemon-lime drink sounded really good. Forget the tea. "Okay."

"Just a sec." He hurried inside. I sat on the porch swing and waited. Moments later he returned with two frosty glasses right out of the freezer and poured the drinks, handing me one before sitting on the rocker beside me. He held up his glass and tapped mine. "To peace."

I didn't return the toast, but I felt more ready to hear what he had to say. The drink was fabulous. Especially after my hot bath.

Toby set his glass down and turned to me. "Lex, hear me out, okay?"

Nodding, I took a deep drink of my shandy.

"I'm really at a loss." He concentrated on my face then shook his head and looked down. "God, how I wish I could turn back time." He took a deep breath and began again. "I will do whatever it takes for you to forgive me. Anything. Just say the word."

I took another drink to hide my eyes. I didn't want him to see me cry. It was frustrating to have all this hurt inside and know that there was not one darned thing anyone could do about it except for me.

"That's just the thing, Toby. I don't know. I'm going to have to learn how to let it go. But I just don't know how."

He held up a dried maple leaf. "Miss Cladie told me about that little girl, Junie. She said the girl grabbed a bunch of leaves off the tree, tearing them away from their intended purpose, to feed the tree. But when they lay on the ground they would decay and still feed the tree in another way."

How many shandies had he imbibed and where was he going with this?

"She told me that I started as a healer, but I'd been stripped from being a doctor. She said I could still be a healer though, by speaking to men about my experience, warning them about temptation and what I lost."

He placed the leaf in my hands. "Maybe you can help others find a way to forgive and love again when you've figured it out. At least that would be a good goal. Shutting the door on the past and moving forward?"

Wow. I studied him. "Did you come home before the girls left?" He had to be eavesdropping.

Stop it, Lexi!

"No, I came back when Avalee got home. When I walked inside, I smelled lavender and figured you were in the bath. Why?"

"Oh." I sipped my shandy. "No reason." I twirled the leaf stem between my fingers. "Toby? Why did you do it? I don't want to hear what a fool you were and all of that." I turned and met his eyes. "But why?"

His face reddened and he looked down at his hands.

"I guess you could say I lost my way. My tunnel vision blinded me to you, our home, and friends. I wasn't looking for another woman. I swear. But when

Claire flattered my over-the-hill ego and continually sent me texts of her naked body, I fell down the rabbit hole. After I was with her, I felt nothing but shame. Every time on my way home, I promised to end it, and not say anything to anyone. But she kept sending pictures more explicit than the ones before and I caved. My guilt put a wall between us." He took a sip of his drink. "Being arrested is what it took, I guess."

I stared off in the dark and listened to night-bug song. He was right. Before the divorce we had become more like roommates, and it wasn't entirely all his doing.

"I have another confession to make."

Oh Lord. I drained my glass and held it out for another.

After he filled it, he said, "Please don't say anything until I finish, okay?"

I nodded and lifted my glass for another gulp.

"Lex, I'm sterile."

Wait. What?

"Remember that time when I had prostatitis? The doc ran a lot of tests and found I had a very low sperm count. Practically nil. But he did say it could happen. He clarified it would be a bit of a miracle. This prognosis gave me hope that there might be a chance. I hung onto that slight possibility and told myself that I wasn't really keeping anything from you. But I wasn't so confident when we talked about trying for a child. Lexi, I was so afraid that you'd change toward me, that my sterility would come between us, so I made excuses about it not being the right time."

It all started to make sense. What he didn't know is that I quit taking the pill so we could have an "accident." But the accident never happened.

He bowed his head and massaged his forehead with his fingertips. "You know, it isn't only women who can feel like biological failures." He caught my gaze with his painful stare. "I wanted to tell you, but my pride just got in the way."

I felt my hardness soften. Yes, he lied. But what about me? Tossing those pills in secret?

He laid his head back against the swing. "When Claire told me she was pregnant, the first thought that came to my mind was, *of all the terrible timing for a miracle*. But it wasn't a miracle. The child wasn't mine."

The night air cooled and the crickets' and tree frogs' songs harmonized in the darkness. I closed my eyes and let Toby's confession sink in. The child wasn't his. He was infertile. He always had been. He didn't tell me for fear I'd lose respect or love for him. Adoption had never crossed his mind. That saddened me more than it irritated me.

Toby went on to explain the rest of the story about Claire, her boyfriend, and her idea for a way to keep her baby. But she had to give her up anyway. Two years later, maturity and her new-found faith helped her understand the horrible thing she'd done. She visited him in prison and confessed it all.

I felt indignation burn in my chest. "What did you say?"

"I told her I forgave her."

"But she left a free woman and you stayed in prison."

"Lex, I was far from innocent. I sinned against you and I took advantage of her. She invited me, but if I'd been the man I should have been, I would have refused the temptation and gone home to you instead."

For the first time I felt pity for him. And for that stupid girl, too. She knew what she was doing, but she had no idea of the consequences her actions meant to anyone else—such as, breaking up my marriage.

It sobered me when I realized he was actually the better person. I had a choice to make. I could remain bitter, or I could become better.

All through the weekend Toby and I walked a delicate line. He wasn't intrusive and I constantly guarded my mind by telling myself the truth. And I had to admit, life felt better.

Sunday morning, he surprised me by walking out all spiffed up and telling me he was going to church with Miss Cladie.

"Say what?" Talk about whiplash.

"I'm going to church with Miss Cladie. Wanna come?"

"Um, no. You go on."

"All right. Suit yourself." He winked. "I'll say a prayer for you."

I smacked his arm. "Get on outta here."

He chuckled and headed out the door. I watched him out the window as he whistled down the street. Now that the burden of his offenses had been admitted and dealt with, he seemed lighter even though he knew he didn't have much time left. That was a sobering thought because no one really knows how much time they have left. I could die before him.

Right then and there, I decided to start savoring life. And I began by heating up that last orange roll.

Chapter Eight

The problem with lust is that it's like cotton candy. It's sweet but quickly dissolves.

The first week of October arrived and brought with it cool nights that hinted of fall. Summer still refused to back off during the day, but this evening had a delightful nip in it and put me in a better mood. It made me feel generous, so much so that I even invited Toby to sit on the front porch with me after the sun set.

Our conversation over wine was philosophical, reflecting over the true meaning of life. I liked that much better than trying to untangle the past. His reflections made me think about my life. I had not yet arrived at that peaceful place he found himself, but the more he spoke, the more I wanted to find it.

Toby held up his glass. "More wine?"

"Sure, but should you be drinking more wine?"

"Hey, it's not like alcohol is going to kill me. That's already taken care of. I might as well enjoy my ride into the sunset." He raised his empty glass and walked inside.

That was a sobering thought. He had decided against treatment, instead, opting for quality of life. I really couldn't blame him, but I didn't know if I could follow that same path.

Toby rejoined me on the porch just as my phone

rang. I checked the screen. Nate.

"Hey, Nate."

"How's my sweet taste of Southern hospitality?"

"Fine and dandy." I glanced up at Toby and took the proffered glass, then mouthed, thank you. Toby lifted his glass and waved goodbye before turning to go back inside.

"And how is my tall, dark, and Yankee?"

"I'll be better next week, say next Tuesday?"

I did the mental calendar. Five days. "Perfect."

"How are things going with the inmate?"

"Rough few months, but it is smoothing out."

"Where is he staying when I'm there?"

"Here. But don't worry. I laid down the law when he first arrived. He won't be any bother."

"Uh, huh."

"Really, he won't. Don't waste your bad boy mind on Toby one minute. Just think about me…about us…and, well, you know."

"Can I change the date of my arrival to…like say…tomorrow?"

"Absolutely not, shug. Ladies on the south-side of fifty need time to spruce up. You men would never understand. I've decided that Mother Nature likes her sons best. Y'all just get better with age."

My boss, Vince, flashed in my mind's eye. Bulging belly, bald head with a sparse circle of hair from one ear to the other, and sagging jowls. "Well, most of you."

"Can't he go to Miss Cladie's and stay? I kinda like my freedom and the little games we play."

"Don't worry. We'll be fine."

Nate sighed. "I just hope he isn't shocked when I

chase you all over the house with nothing on but my personality."

"Maybe you better get here tonight."

He gave a soft chuckle. "Night, Red."

"Night. See you soon."

I clicked off my phone and thought about the freedom Nate and I always enjoyed in my home. It would feel strange with Toby here. Maybe he should go to Molly's.

I'd think on that tomorrow.

****

Tuesday finally arrived. Nate called to say he'd rented a hot little car and that he'd pick me up from work around four. I dreaded telling Vince because he always drooled over Nate. It was downright embarrassing. But tell him I must. I stepped on the elevator and practiced my most breezy, nonchalant announcement. My plan was to briefly stick my head in, tell him, and then make a run for it down the exit steps.

Vince had his back to me when I peeked through the cracked door. "Hey, Vince. I'm taking off early because Na—"

Before I got Nate's name from my mouth Vince whirled around in his chair, stood, and ran to the door. The mention of Nate's name turned my overweight, exercise-challenged boss into an Olympic champion.

"When's he coming? How long is he staying? Do you think he'd have a beer with me?"

I put up my hands. "Whoa, Vince. He is coming to see me. Maybe, if there's time, we can work something out." I held up my finger. "But I'm not promising anything."

Vince pulled a handkerchief from his back pocket and wiped his forehead. “How do I look? Do I need to change shirts?”

This was pitiful. I’d never seen a straight guy with such a man-crush. “He isn’t coming in. He said for me to meet him outside because he had a surprise for me.”

Vince’s shoulders sagged. I actually felt sorry for him. “But maybe tomorrow. We can all have coffee or something like that.”

He brightened up. “That would be fantastic.”

“Okay, well, I need to freshen up before he gets here.”

“Good, I was going to suggest that.” Vince turned back toward his desk.

Excuse me? I hurried to the bathroom and stared in the mirror. I’d taken extra time getting ready that morning. All I needed was a little powder and lipstick. I had my hair color refreshed to hide the gray hairs that invaded my hairline. I might be a bit curvier from stress eating. Damn it. Vince and his jealous little digs. He’d make a great teenaged mean girl.

My phone chimed. It was Nate texting me that he was at the front door of the office. I hurried out to find him in a cherry-red convertible. He leaned over and opened the door. I slid onto the seat and into his arms. We gave everyone within eyeshot something to talk about. The desire hadn’t left me. It was still there pounding away.

“Good to see you, Red.”

“I thought you’d never get here.” I took a second to study Nate. Something was different. He’d grown a beard. Both his hair and beard were the most delicious salt and pepper. I fingered his beard. “When did this happen?"

"I've been investigating for an assignment, so I thought I'd let it grow out since there's no camera time." He ran his fingers through his mop of wind-blown hair. Definitely more salt than pepper. Again, Mother Nature and her sons. Geeze. And to think how I had worried about my few gray hairs. Men. They just let it go and feel great about themselves. What is wrong with us women? Mollie Kate excepted. That girl rocked confidence in her plus size figure.

"Now, about that surprise." He gave me a wicked smile. "Put on your seatbelt and hold tight." He pulled onto the street and raced two blocks, turned left onto Leslie Lane and right on Nightingale, then onto Molly Kate's bed and breakfast parking lot.

"Why are we at Molly Kate's?"

"We have a room here."

"But…"

He put his finger to my mouth. "No arguments. I'll only be here a couple of days and I want it to be just us. Staying at your house isn't an option."

"But I was going to send Toby here."

"No need. I have our room all ready. In fact, there won't be a reason to leave it."

"As tempting as that sounds, I need to at least pack something."

He winked. "No, you don't."

"Well, I *do* need my toothbrush." I noticed Molly Kate peeking from the window. "Let's go in and get MK's million unasked questions over with."

Nate jumped out of the car, which was impressive for a man in his sixties, and opened my door. "Go on in and answer questions. I'll grab my bag and be in soon."

Molly met me at the door.

I felt embarrassed, like a guilty teenager. I took in a breath. “Hey.”

“Hey, yourself.” Molly Kate winked.

“Did you know about this?”

Before she could answer he walked beside me. “We meet again, Molly Kate.”

“We sure do, handsome. I have your suite ready, complete with champagne on ice.”

I raised my eyebrows. “Wow.”

He grinned. “The best for the best.”

“Well, before we pop the cork, I really do need a few things.”

“Let’s get settled in first.” He gave me his best little boy pout.

“Nope.” I turned him around and slapped his fanny.

Molly took his duffel bag. “I’ll take this. Y’all go on.”

In no time we were back on Leslie Lane speeding toward Washington Avenue. And as far as I was concerned, he couldn’t go fast enough.

****

From the minute that little red convertible pulled in the driveway, Toby knew he did not like Nathan Wolfe. If only he’d been the man he should have been, she’d be with him, not that Nathan guy.

Nathan waited in the car while she ran inside and into her room. Toby followed her. “Well, isn’t he coming in?”

“No.” She slung an overnight case on her bed then hurried to the bathroom. “We are staying at the Norton B&B.”

"We?"

She came out with a handful of toiletries, threw them in her bag, turned and pointed her finger at him.

"Don't start. Remember the rules?"

"Yeah, I remember." There was so much he wanted to say—hell—that he wanted to scream. *You are worth more than being his plaything. He is using you. Don't be a fool.* But he couldn't because he, Toby Lowe, had been just as bad.

Lexi pulled a few things out of her dresser, threw them in her case, and hurried to the door.

"See you in a couple of days Toby. If you need anything call Miss Cladie or Sid. Bye."

Toby lifted his hand in a half-hearted wave and watched her get in the sportscar. Nathan looked at Toby and pulled Lexi close. His message was clear. Lexi was his.

The next two days were agonizing. Toby wandered around the house remembering happier days. To say he was miserable was an understatement. He made himself a glass of iced tea and walked to the back patio. Being outside always helped clear his mind. Just as he slunk down on the patio glider, his phone pinged. It was Lex. He sucked in a breath and read.

Hey, just want you to know I'll be home tomorrow after work.

As if on their own, his lips curved into a smile. That Wolfe guy was leaving and hopefully it would be months before he returned. Which would probably leave her in low spirits.

Just then, he had an idea. He'd do his best to cheer her up. She'd come home to a sparkling house, flowers, and her favorite Italian dinner. Before he grabbed an

Uber to the Piggly Wiggly store, he stared up through the tree branches and offered a quick prayer. "Lord, please send Nate to the other side of the world on a story that will last at least a year."

He knew this was selfish and wouldn't happen. Even so, it felt good to pray it.

****

Nate was about to leave, and as much as it puzzled me to feel this, I was glad. The whole visit felt so awkward. Here we are at Molly Kate's shacking up like two teenagers in a hotel. I also understood him not wanting to be at my house. This should have stirred my anger at Toby for messing up my life. But somehow, I couldn't blame him either. Something just wasn't right.

While he showered, I went to Molly Kate's house that adjoined the B&B and walked into her kitchen. Molly and Stan were sitting at the table drinking coffee. Sadness tugged my heart. I missed the daily routines of being a couple.

"Well, good morning, sugar." Molly stood and walked to the coffee maker. "Get any sleep last night?" Her eyebrows pumped up and down. I felt nothing but embarrassment, but I covered it up with my go to—sarcasm.

"Not a bit. We were two owls hooting until dawn." Which wasn't exactly true.

Stan stood. "Aaaannnd this is where I leave you girls to your chat." He kissed Molly, patted my shoulder, and left to prepare breakfast for the *other* guests.

Molly set a cup of coffee in front of me. "When does Nate leave?"

"In about an hour. I'll go to work late so I can see

him off." I blew the steam off my coffee and took a sip. "He said he had something important to ask me."

"He did?" Molly's jaw dropped. "Lord've mercy."

I waved her off. "It's not that." *But what if it was?*

What do you think it is then?"

"I haven't the foggiest." *If it was a proposal, what would I say?*

We chatted a little longer. I'm not sure what we talked about because my mind was filled with Molly's assumption.

"Well, MK, I'd better get back to the room. He is probably dressed by now."

Molly stood. "Girl, you better give me a call the minute—and I mean the *very* minute—he gets in that cute little car and drives off."

"I will."

I found Nate sitting on the bed tying his shoe. He looked up and smiled. "Where have you been?"

"Coffee with MK."

He patted the spot beside him. "Come here, I have something, a favor, to ask."

Well, marriage proposals were certainly not favors. I felt a little disappointed. "What's that?'

"November third, I'm receiving an achievement award for journalism. It's kind of a big deal. And I need a date." He took my hand. "Would you be that date, Red?"

I put my hand to my chest. "Me?"

"Yeah. You."

"But why me? There are so many other more…" I threw my hands up in the air. "Oh, I don't know, *sophisticated* women, *younger* women who would look better by your side. I take horrible pictures. I'd look like a cow on television. Face it, I'm not your best PR choice."

"Don't worry about that. The cameras would focus on me. And all of my colleagues will be crowded around. All you have to do is smile. And when it is all over, I'll take you to a fabulous hotel room and we can continue what we started here."

Millions of excuses filled my mind. I didn't have the right clothes, but Avalee could help me with that. I didn't know how to speak anything but southern, but Jema could help me there, seeing how she sounds almost purely European now. I didn't have confidence, but Molly Kate had that in spades. She could give me a few pointers.

"Earth to Lexi." Nate's eyes crinkled above his smile.

"Oh." I caught myself staring at him like a cat watches a moth before pouncing. "Sorry. Okay. Yes. I'll go."

He leaned in for a kiss. "That's my girl." He rose from the bed and pulled me up with him. "I'll make all the arrangements and email them to you.

Still stunned, I managed to mutter. "Ok. Sounds good."

He pulled me in for a killer goodbye kiss, then whispered against my neck. "Sure, I can't drop you off at work?"

Memories of Vince's behavior the day before when we paid our obligatory visit to satisfy his man-crush, caused me to answer, perhaps a little too hastily, "No." Then I pulled back and smiled. "Unless you want to see your boyfriend again."

He grimaced. "In that case, you'd better walk to

work, Red." He gave me a sweet peck on the cheek and grabbed his duffel. "I'll get back with you soon."

I waved as he hurried down the hall. Unease filled the pit of my stomach. I didn't want to go to Manhattan. I didn't want to hang with his crowd and be a novelty to his Yankee friends.

The very thought about anyone being condescending made the southern girl in me rise up and shake her fist. Yes, I'm southern and proud of it. And I would not be responsible for what would come out of my mouth if some unfortunate soul made fun of me.

I'd better think this out again.

Chapter Nine

You just gotta to know yourself and take a stand.

Molly Kate didn't waste any time hurrying up the stairs as soon as Nate drove off. When she reached the top of the stairs she bent over, clapped her hands to her knees, and gulped air.

"What," deep breath, blowing it out, "did he," deep breath, blowing it out, "say?"

"Let's go to the kitchenette and have a bloody Mary first. Then I'll tell you everything."

Molly Kate stood and took another deep breath, then let it out. "Day drink? Is it that bad?"

"No, not really. But I'm scared to death."

We went to the second story kitchen that she and Stan had installed for guests to enjoy snacks and drinks. In the cupboard were glasses, dishes, and cutlery. There was also a microwave, ice machine, and fridge. Hidden from view was a liquor cabinet for entertaining.

Molly Kate unlocked the cabinet and took out a bottle of vodka and poured a jigger full into two tall glasses. Then she added spiced tomato juice, a splash of Worcestershire, and ice. We went back to my room and plopped on the couch. She held her glass up and clinked mine. "Cheers. Now spill."

After a long drink I said, "He wants me to be his date at an event in New York the first Friday night of

November."

MK scrunched up her face. "Aaannnd that's bad, how?"

I turned to her. "Are you kidding me? New York City! There will be cameras, television, I'll be on world news."

"Okay, help me here. I'm not picking up what you're putting down."

I stood. "Look at me. I'm barely over five feet, my five pounds overweight looks like fifty, I'm almost fifty-nine for heaven's sakes." I slunk down next to Molly and laid my head on her shoulder. "Besides, I'm not smart enough to be around his crowd."

"Oh, pshaw." Molly patted my hand. "I've heard you say a lot of dumb things, but this one takes home the prize."

I held up my glass. "Just one more? Then I can face Vince."

Molly was as quick as a hiccup with our drinks. She handed mine to me and said, "You remember how y'all got me all fixed up to meet Stan? Well, I'm calling in the troops for operation Lexi, destination New York." I did remember. Ava was her stylist, I did her hair, Jema applied her makeup, and all of us reeled in her sinking confidence. "You will look ahh-mazin. Besides, Nate wants you there. *That* is enough reason to go."

She was right, of course. And I have to admit, after her assurance of help and two shots of vodka, I did feel better. Even good enough to face Vince and listen about his man-crush for the rest of the afternoon. *Lord help me...*

****

After work, I walked into my house and the most delicious aromas engulfed me. Toby met me with a glass of my favorite wine.

"Welcome home." His smile was genuine, if a little sad. "I'm making us dinner. I hope you don't mind."

"Is that what I think it is?"

His smile widened, "Lasagna, bread smothered in garlic butter, and a crisp Caesar salad. And for dessert, tiramisu.

Frank Sinatra's music floated through the room and into the kitchen. It was so…so…right. My mind time-traveled back twenty years when we were together. When we were happy. I took a sip of cabernet. "This is nice, Toby. But I can't…we can't…"

He put his hand up. "No, I get it. But we can still be friends and have fun. Make special moments. Right?"

"Yes, that we can do."

"I'm also going to grill some whole onions—"

"—stuffed with butter and garlic?" I felt like an excited little girl.

"The very thing." All the sadness had left his smile. "Why don't you take a hot bath and relax. The lasagna will be ready soon, and when you get out, I'll toast the garlic bread."

"Okay, that sounds fabulous." He refilled my glass and walked behind the kitchen counter. "I'm glad you're back."

"Me too." And I was. The past few days had been wearisome. To be honest, I was happy to be home and that Nate was back in New York. I was also glad that Toby respected my privacy and didn't mention or ask anything about the past couple of days.

I ran a tubful of hot water, poured in a generous amount of bubble bath, and slipped in. While I relaxed, I wondered if I should talk with Toby about New York. He used to be my go-to when I was troubled. Could we be that again? I put that thought out of my mind. For now, I'd let the silky scented water do its magic.

Toby had the table set and ready when I walked into the dining room. "All finished?"

"Yes, and it was fabulous. Thank you."

"Refill your glass and go sit on the porch. I'll call when the bread is ready."

He didn't have to twist my arm. I poured more wine and strolled to the porch. It felt fantastic outside. Summer had finally lost its grasp. The evening air was cool and soft. I sat on the porch swing and toed it back and forth while mentally decorating for fall using the pumpkins I'd get from Miss Cladie's garden.

A few minutes later Toby stuck his head out the door. "Dinner's ready."

"I'll be right in." Life here. It was good. I decided to quit looking back with regret. Instead, I'd keep a forward focus. And ahead of me was a great meal.

I don't know what got into me, but I ate every bite on my plate and then had seconds. Seconds! Toby handed me more cabernet. "Wanna sit on the porch for a while?"

"Sounds lovely."

He hesitated, then asked, "May I join you?"

"Yeah." Nostalgia gave me the courage to say, "There's something I want to talk to you about anyway." The moment I said it I felt that I might have made a poor choice. After all, you don't plant kudzu in your vegetable patch, and you don't talk to your ex-husband about your boyfriend.

Oh well, I might as well go for it.

The evening air felt like velvet—warm and soft against my skin. Toby sat next to me and for a while we just rocked back and forth, sipping while listening to the subdued autumn song of the remaining katydids. A few fireflies still lingered, twinkling in the darkness like dancing fairies. I relaxed in my decision to talk to Toby.

"So," he turned to me, "what did you want to talk about?"

"Actually, Nate." I watched for his reaction. A flinch? Outright disgust? But saw nothing.

"Okay, shoot." He looked genuinely interested.

"He wants me to be his escort for some kind of award he is getting."

"Is that a problem?"

"I don't know." I lifted my glass to my lips pondering why I felt so uncomfortable. "I just don't feel like I'd fit in with his crowd."

"Lex, you fit in anywhere. You can talk to anyone about anything." He patted my knee. "So, what is really bothering you?"

He read me like a winning lottery ticket.

"I guess the truth is, maybe, I don't *want* to fit in."

The past week made me feel strange. Shacking up at Molly's B & B. All the other times when Nate came to visit me in my home, our time together seemed natural. But to go across town felt cheap. Besides, I didn't feel like exposing myself to celebrities who tried to talk southern in their films and sounded like idiots doing it. I didn't want to worry about how to look, how to act, what to wear. And Nate? How would he change in *his* crowd? He willingly entered mine and endured

Vince. But I wasn't so sure I could do the same.

"Are you afraid you might embarrass him, and he'd break up with you?"

"Not really." I stared off into the darkness. "What I don't understand is, he could have any number of women so why me?"

Toby voice fell. "Maybe he loves *you*." His statement dropped with a thud. Impossible. No way. Not in a million years. "What if he does?"

"I don't know. I truly don't."

"Do you love him?" There was a tiny crack in Toby's voice when he asked.

"I care about him, but," I glanced up and whispered, "I don't think I know how to love anymore."

Toby grimaced, cleared his throat and stood. "More?"

I pinched my fingers together. "Just a smidge."

"Be right back."

What in blue blazes was wrong with me? Toby's words sat like a brick in my stomach. Did I want Nate to love me? I had loved Toby with every fiber of my being. When I learned of his betrayal, I'd never hurt so bad in my life and it wasn't just a few months pain. It still hurt. But I'd learned to live with it. Even though I'd forgiven Toby, the scar remained.

Could I love again? Trust again?

Toby returned, handed me my glass, and sat next to me on the swing. "I can't believe I'm about to say this."

Well, that got my attention.

"I think you should go."

"What? Why?"

"So you can be sure about Nate. About yourself."

The chain on the swing creaked as we swayed. "I can't see me loving anyone again. Not the marrying kind of love."

Toby's glance flickered over me with the same painful look he got when I said I didn't know if I could love again, but he didn't say anything.

"I think I'll go on to go to bed. Thanks for a great dinner." I put my hand on his arm. "And for the pleasant evening. It's been nice to have someone to bounce things off of."

His expression had darkened, but he smiled. "My pleasure. Night."

I paced to my room. I needed time and space to think. It was going to be a long night.

Chapter Ten

Lust has an expiration date. Who knew?

After Lexi went to bed, Toby decided to give the kitchen a good cleaning. There was no way he'd be able to sleep with thoughts racing around his mind like in a speedway.

Had he ruined her chance at happiness should it ever present itself? *Had* he already ruined her relationship to Nate? It hurt to hear her say she didn't know if she could love again. The guilt weighed on his soul. It was all his fault.

He stacked the dishes, rinsed them, and arranged them in the dishwasher. The repetitive movement and Tetris placement of the dishes to achieve maximum use of space helped him to focus. If only he knew how to make things right, how to help her love again.

If only she could love him again.

He shook his head at this thought. It wouldn't be fair. To try and win her love back would be yet another selfish act on his part. He had no idea how much longer he had on this earth. Still, to have Lexi love him again, well, a man could dream, couldn't he?

****

Toby threw a wrench—no—the whole dadgumed toolbox in the conversation when he said that Nate might possibly love me.

Did he love me?

I wasn't sure how I felt about that. Did I love him? The past few years had been great. Keeping up through phone calls and email made seeing him once or twice a year thrilling. Our passion flared into flames. That is, until this last visit. Something had changed.

Even though Toby suggested I go, in my gut I knew that was a bad idea. I had to go with my intuition. I would not be going to New York. Now, how in the heck to tell Nate?

****

Three weeks had passed and not a word from Nathan. Wasn't he cutting the travel arrangements pretty close? On the other hand, I should have already contacted him to say I wasn't coming. I kept wimping out. Still, why hadn't he called me?

I needed to talk. I needed my friends. Even though it was late, I dialed Molly Kate.

"Hey, Lex." Molly's voice was thick with sleep. "Something wrong?"

"Hey. Hon, I'm sorry for calling so late, but I need to talk. To all of you. Can we have a Whine Wednesday at your place this week?"

"Yeah. Sure." Her voice cleared and tinged with worry. "What's up?"

"Let's talk about it Wednesday. It isn't anything bad, I just need y'all's input. I'll text Avalee and Jema."

"Okay, night, sugar."

"Night."

I texted the girls and heard back from both of them right away. Both asking what was wrong to which I answered, *we will talk Wednesday.*

I could hardly wait to drink wine and whine to the

girls who knew me best and accepted me as I was. Lord, I loved my friends.

****

Wednesday night finally arrived. The wait had been miserable. My mind just wouldn't stop with the what ifs, why nots, hows, and if onlys. Every scenario jungle-gymed in my head. Frankly, by the time I got to Molly Kate's, I was worn out mentally and physically.

When she swung open the door, right away, I smelled my favorite snacks. God love her.

I handed her a bottle of bourbon.

"That bad, huh?"

"Yep."

"Come in. I made your favs."

That's one of the many great things about southern women. We feed each other. If you're sad, here's all the fat and carbs you can eat to elevate your mood. Sick? Here's some soup. Someone pass? Bring that family fried chicken or a casserole. Celebrating? Have some cake. Bored? Let's get ice cream.

"I hope the bacon I smell is wrapped around a cream cheese stuffed date."

"Yep, everything I made for tonight is just the way you like it, savory and sweet."

"Did you make those cranberry brie puffs?"

"Yes, ma'am."

My mouth began to water. I hadn't been able to eat all day. "I feel better already." I followed her to the kitchen just itching to sample those puffs.

A knock came at the kitchen door and Avalee stuck her head in. "Hey, girls."

Molly took Avalee's wine, white as always.

"Momma loaded me up with goodies. Lend a

hand?" I followed her to the car. Miss Cladie had outdone herself and that's a good thing seeing how the extent of Ava's cooking skills were limited to reading a menu. Good thing Ava and Ty lived with Miss Cladie or the man would starve.

"Momma made you a coconut cake, she knows how much you love them." Avalee handed me the cake carrier. Oh. My. Word. I was at the point of drooling. Miss Cladie always made her cake masterpiece using three layers of soft cake soaked in coconut syrup and iced in the most decadent cream cheese, buttercream frosting, finished off with tender, sweet coconut shreds. I was ready to dive into it face first.

Ava gave a tray to Molly, "And she fried up some onion rings. Another of Lex's favorites."

Molly glanced at the last covered platter. "And I suppose that is something healthy for you."

"Nope. Pulled pork sliders with horseradish sauce."

I put my hand up. "Okay, just stop. My stomach sounds like there's a thunderstorm brewing."

"Yoo-hoo." Jema came sailing into the kitchen carrying a long board draped with a checkered towel. After she set it on the table, she yanked it off. "Two years in Italy have definitely changed my *foodie* style." On the board was a variety of soft and hard cheeses, olives, grapes, dates, assortment of nuts, crusty bread, jams, and prosciutto. "Plus, the perfect paring." She set two bottles of Chianti beside it.

"Girls, I think that after we eat and drink all of this, I'll have no problems at all." I patted my stomach. "Except for maybe being able to fit into my jeans."

"This is a lot of food." Avalee picked up a plate. "I hate the thought of it going to waste."

"No worries." Molly Kate slapped her hands together. "After we eat all we can, I'll serve what's left to my guests." She nodded her head toward food. "Let's fill our plates and head to the library for our whine."

"Hello, ladies." Molly's hubby sauntered into the kitchen. "Sure smells good in here. If I can think of a whine, will I be permitted to partake of this feast?"

"Feast, yes, whine, no. Girls only. But…" Molly lowered her head and peered up at him. "if you take all this wine to the library, I'll make it worth your while later…"

Stan grabbed the bottles. "Done."

"And," said Molly Kate, "you'd better eat hearty. You'll need your strength."

That man moved like a racehorse crossing the finish line. By the time we got to the library, he'd set up fresh glasses, had the white wine on ice, and decanted the red wine. I settled in one of the buttery-soft leather chairs and sipped my cold, crisp, chardonnay.

This room was a classic. Built-in shelves filled with books formed two walls, complete with a ladder that rolled in front of each in order to reach the volumes ten feet up. A massive marble fireplace was built in a third wall where a portrait of Mr. and Mrs. Norton, former owners of the mansion, looked down on us. The fourth wall was the bar area covered in rich mahogany paneling. Behind the bar was an ornate mirror with small accent lights on either side creating a soothing ambience.

I wiggled my toes in the lush, deep-pile rug and took another sip. What a shame to ruin this lovely evening with problems. Still, that was why we were all here. My stomach grumbled, reminding me that it was impatient for food. I surveyed my overflowing plate. Miss Cladie's onion rings were my first choice. I picked up a perfectly fried, golden-brown ring and bit into the lightly salted, crispy crust and the tender, sweet onion. Ahhhhhh, heaven. My tastebuds sang with gratitude.

Avalee held up her glass of Chianti. "Jema, this makes me want to go back to Italy."

Jema smiled, "I guess you could say that is my whine. I miss Levi. But I'm also ready to move home. These past two years have been beyond my greatest dreams, but this southern gal misses her roots."

I bit into a warm, creamy brie and cranberry tart. Its flaky layers melted on my tongue. *Yum*. "How long will you be here?"

"I'm leaving in a couple of weeks." She popped an olive in her mouth. "But we will be back soon." She turned to Molly Kate who sat on the sofa next to her. "Now are you sure it won't be a problem for us living here? It could take a year or longer."

"Course not." Molly pointed her bacon wrapped date at Jema. "Sakes. What a thing to ask. I've been thinking," she took a bite, "you know the perfect place for y'all?" Another bite. "The pool house."

"Perfect," said Avalee. "That's a great idea."

"It has a nice kitchen, big bathroom, spacious living room and a large bedroom. By staying there, you won't always be bumping into guests in the mansion. And if folks are in the pool, just close the blinds." Molly brushed her hands together. "The bedroom is in the back and has a sweet little patio where you can sit and have some privacy. I just hope the living space isn't too small for you since the villa."

"You know, it's funny," Jema smiled. "But we

only live in three rooms there. The rest is unused. I love being out in the gardens there, but you have fantastic gardens here."

"As far as I'm concerned," I lifted my empty glass, "The sooner the better."

Avalee laughed, "For Jema to come home or for your glass to be filled?"

"Both!" I stood and pulled the bottle out of the ice. "Anyone else need a refill?"

Everyone held up their glass.

After our glasses were filled, Avalee sighed. "I guess I'll confess my whine."

We were all ears.

"I don't like the grandma name Skye chose for me." She twisted her lip. "Granny."

Oh. My. Lord. Images of the bespeckled granny toting a shot gun in Beverly Hills shot across my mind. I burst out laughing. Karma! That's what it was. Our divinely beautiful, never-aging friend, being called *granny*.

Jema had her hand over her mouth trying to look sympathetic, but Molly Kate laid her head back and roared.

"It's not funny." Avalee tried to not smile. "It's not." Soon she laughed as hard as the rest of us.

When we all got a grip on ourselves, Molly Kate palmed her eyes and asked, "What did you say when she told you that?"

"I told her, 'Thank you, but I think I'll name myself if you don't mind.'"

Jema patted her lashes with her shirttail. "What did she say?"

"She said I had to run my ideas by her first, and I

said, remember who is going to pay for your wedding, your graduation party, and your honeymoon. To which she said, 'Give yourself whatever name you like.'"

The pulled pork slider was just begging for me to eat it. I picked it up and asked, "Any ideas what you want to be called?" Then I bit into the sweet, smoky richness.

She put her finger to her chin and gazed up at the ceiling. "I'm thinking shug."

"Oh lord, Avalee." Molly Kate shook her head. "The child will start calling you slug. Think of something the child can pronounce easy. Something like Grammy or Mimi?"

Jema chimed in, "Or Nonni?"

"All good suggestions." Ava nestled back into the pillows. "I'll give it more thought. Molly Kate? Any whines?"

"None to speak of unless it is meeting myself coming and going. Between the shop and the B&B, Stan and I are too exhausted to even blow a kiss to each other much less anything else."

"Which," I grinned, "explains his eagerness to help tonight."

"Oh, hush up." Molly's cheeks rosied up. "Your turn, Lex. Let's have it."

I held my finger up. "First." I stood, walked to the bar, and grabbed a low-ball glass, then dropped in two cubes of ice and poured an ounce of bourbon over them. "Girls, I need your help." I drained the glass.

They all sat looking at me with rounded eyes. Molly put her hand to her chest. "Lord, Lex. What?"

I plopped back onto my chair. "I'm done."

Ava leaned forward with an impatient splay of

hands, "With what?"

"Nate."

"Lordamercy, Lex? What in heaven's name are you talking about?" Molly Kate frowned. "You seemed all right on his last visit."

"And that's when I started getting this feeling that something wasn't right." I stood to get another bourbon. "So much has happened in such a short time. I guess you could say I've had a paradigm shift."

Jema chimed in. "You have been through a lot lately, sugar. What with Toby returning and living in your house."

This time I sipped my drink. "Toby's changed. He's turning back into the man I married—thoughtful, sweet, and totally into me." Another sip. "And he's dying."

"So, are you saying you've forgiven him?"

I smiled at Molly. "Yeah. I had to make that choice or be miserable the rest of my life."

Avalee frowned. "So, is this why you feel differently about Nate?"

"That's just it, Avalee, I don't know. He's asked me to be his escort at some thingamajig in Manhattan, an award he is receiving. I told him I'd go, but really? I'd rather eat liver."

"Just tell him." Avalee grinned. "He will be cool about it. It's not like he can't get a date seconds after you bow out."

I threw a pillow at her. "Can't you let me think I'm irreplaceable for just one hot second?"

She laughed. "I said he could get a date, not that he'd enjoy being with anyone but you."

"There's got to be a graceful way out." Jema stared

off in thought. But she didn't have to think long because my phone rang. I froze, thinking it was Nate. I wasn't ready to talk to him. Thankfully Sid's name showed on the screen. The girls must have been thinking the same thing by the way they all stared at me.

"It's Sid." I walked out of the room before I answered. "Hey, Sid. What's up?"

"I have good news. Audy made a spot for us on his calendar to talk about the factory reno. The afternoon of November third. Are you free on that date?"

I lifted my face heavenward and mouthed, "Thank you, Jesus," then said, "Absolutely."

When the call was finished, I sashayed back into the room. "I have my excuse."

Molly followed up behind me holding Miss Cladie's cake. "Well, that was quick."

"What is it?" asked Jema.

"Well, you know we have plans for the old hosiery factory and the only time our architect can meet with us is the first Friday of November. Well, I'm a principle in the meeting, so I can't be Nate's date." I took a thick slice of cake and ate a bite. In that moment, with tender coconut-infused cake enveloped in sweet, creamy frosting on my tongue, all was right with the world. I could conquer anything. But I knew when the cake euphoria evaporated, I'd have to call Nate. I had some explaining to do.

The evening spent with my besties gave me the courage I needed to make *the call*. I felt both relieved and bad. After they left, I checked the clock. Ten. Eleven o'clock his time. He'd still be up and besides, I wanted to get this over with. I speed dialed his number.

A soft, breathy, Marilyn Monroe-like voice answered his phone. "Hello?"

"Um." *what the?* I fought to clear my head. "Is Nate there?"

"Sure." The voice whispered, "Nathan. It's for you." Apparently, they were close together. Really close.

I heard Nate heave a sigh, and then, "Hello Red."

"Hey? Did I interrupt something?"

He hesitated, then said, "Nothing that can't be finished later. What's up?"

Finished later? Fire ants crawled in my veins. What the hell?

"Red? Are you still there?"

"Uh, yeah." Okay, now I sounded like an idiot. I took a deep breath and forged on. "Hey, listen, I'm sorry, but I can't go to the awards ceremony with you. You know that project Sid and I are working on? There is an important meeting on the same day as your ceremony and I just can't miss it." There. I did it. I took a deep breath. "I'm so sorry, hon."

"Okay, no problem."

And that was it? No problem?

"Oookay?"

"It will probably work out better this way, anyway."

Work out better? My southern bitch rose up inside me. "And another thing, I think we need to quit seeing each other." *There, take that Romeo.*

"You know, Red, we must be on the same wave-length. I've been thinking the same thing. It was great while it lasted, but yeah, it's time. Everything has a shelf life."

Great, now I'm a can of green beans to him. It made no sense at all, but I actually felt hurt. Betrayed. He was getting it on with Miss Breathy Voice and considered me expired.

"Okay then. See you in the news." Before I said something I would regret, I hung up. And I actually cried, for heaven's sake.

Toby had just returned from Miss Cladie's and heard me. "Lex, what's wrong?"

I didn't want to talk about it, then again, I did. But it felt strange talking to my ex-husband about my now ex-lover.

"Nate." I swiped away tears. "We broke up."

To his credit, he didn't try to console me. Instead, he sat beside me on the sofa and waited.

"I'm so stupid. Why would he ever want some unsophisticated southern hick? He's such a jerk." I planted my chin in my hands. "I thought we were an item, a couple, even though neither of us ever made it official."

Toby handed me a tissue.

"I don't know why I'm letting it affect me like this."

"Because another jerk did the very same thing to you years ago." His voice grew tight. "Something that I'd give my life to change."

Sitting beside him in what used to be *our* living room and having him comfort me, like he used to do, made me wish we *could* begin again. He wasn't the handsome man of years ago, but over the past few weeks as I watched him through the lens of forgiveness rather than bitterness, he'd grown more handsome in his soul. As I told the girls, he'd returned to be the man

I married. And right then, I wanted his arms around me. I wanted to sink against him.

As if he had read my mind, he pulled me toward him, and I rested my head against his chest.

This felt right. Like it always should have been.

****

Toby rose early the next morning and showered. The warm water flowed over him, a luxury he'd always taken for granted before prison. It was too bad that it took dying to make him appreciate life. He lifted his face to the spray. Never did he ever think he would hold Lexi in his arms again.

Miracles did happen.

But where would things go from here? He stepped out of the shower and scrubbed with a towel. It was best to take his cues from her, like he did last night. Was he wrong to hope that she might love him again?

After dressing, he headed to the kitchen. Lex would be up soon, and she liked her coffee fresh.

****

The aroma of coffee wafted into my room. I stretched and threw back the blanket. A soft knock sounded at the door and Toby walked in carrying a mug.

"Morning, babe. Coffee?"

I noted the familiar pet name, *babe*, but that was okay. "Morning and yes. Coffee, right away."

He set the mug on the nightstand. "Take your time and when you are up and about, let's have breakfast and a talk."

"Yeah, I think we need to."

He leaned over and timidly pecked me on the forehead before leaving. It felt nice, especially since my heart still stung from Nate's indifference. It still didn't make sense why Nate's brushoff hurt so bad. And then there was Toby. His quiet strength, and yes, love, kept me afloat.

I just wish I could understand Nate's sudden change of heart. He didn't even talk to me about it. But then, neither did I…but still…

My phone chimed and the screen showed it was the man himself. Jerk.

"What, Nate?"

"Hey, Red, I—"

"My name is Lexi."

"Lex—"

"Lexi. And if you get it wrong again, you can call me Miss Lowe."

"Hey, I get it. You're mad and I don't blame you. I feel like I owe you an explanation."

"Oh really? Astound me."

A heavy sigh sounded before he spoke. "When I got home from your place, I went to dinner with some colleagues and one of them introduced me to a woman, who happens to be the daughter of a major news network executive."

"Was it Miss Breathy Voice who answered your phone?"

"That would be Monica. Yes."

"Go on."

"She and I hit it off and have been seeing each other almost every night."

Every night? Well, why not? Apparently I was expired.

"A couple of evenings ago she told me that her father was working on a primetime news slot and looking for a chief news anchor. She said she'd put in a good word for me."

"Well, la-de-dah for you."

"Red…I mean Lexi, this is big. You've got to understand what this means. She's my ticket."

"Wow, isn't that romantic." I honestly felt sorry for the girl. "Let me guess. The nano-second we hung up you asked her to be your escort."

The phone was silent.

"Okay, well, it was nice knowing you these past few years. Break a leg." And I meant that literally. Before he could answer I disconnected. Then powered my phone off. In a way I was grateful that I was, for the first time, seeing this side of Nathan. I knew, at times, he could be an arrogant ass. But not a player. Is that what he'd been doing with me? Using me?

That thought ticked me off. I strode to the bathroom and grumbled at the image in the mirror, "Somewhere on a bathroom wall in the universe is a message that says, "Dumb redhead. Give her a call."

The aroma of bacon and baking muffins drifted into my room. A balm to my irritated soul. When I shuffled into the kitchen, Toby took one look at me and held his arms open. I rushed into them and released my pent-up tears. He didn't say a word.

In his comforting embrace, I knew, this was how it always should have been.

Chapter Eleven

Miracles do happen!

Thanksgiving was three weeks away and I had a lot to be thankful for. Once again Toby and I were soulmates. It felt right and natural doing life together. Another thing to be thankful for. Sid wanted to hire me full time, so, I was quitting the paper.

Vince will die. I still hadn't told him about me and Nate breaking up. I decided to do that when I handed in my resignation. It might make it easier for him to let me go. Besides, with this huge project of repurposing a hosiery factory into a convention center and a warehouse into a boutique hotel, there was absolutely no time for my column. As Nate had so sensitively put it, *everything has a shelf life.*

"Thanks, Nate," I said to no one. "I'll always think of that when I watch you on television."

Jerk.

I reviewed the bids for the projects. Wow. I knew they would be expensive, but lordy mercy. Our uber-expensive project meant a fight with the town council and I had to be ready for that ornery Jim Fleming. I'd swear, if his brains were dynamite, he couldn't blow his nose.

I didn't have an office at town hall, so sometimes Sid and I worked from my house, which I liked better.

After all, I couldn't be late for work that way. Every now and then, Toby sat in on our meetings. His insight astonished me. Another positive about working from home was how it deepened Sid's and Toby's friendship. Sometimes, while Sid and I worked, Toby made dinner. We've spent many pleasant evenings together.

I hadn't mentioned to anyone about my re-connection with Toby. I chuckled just thinking about the reaction I'd get from the girls.

"What's so funny?" Toby sauntered into the living room holding a plate of chocolate chunk brownies. "Just outta the oven." He sank beside me. "Have one."

"Are you trying to make me fat so no one else will look at me?" I grabbed a brownie.

"You found me out." He grinned. "Now you know my evil plan."

The brownies were delicious. Warm, moist, with that nice creamy bite of melting chocolate. "Well, it's not like anyone will look at this graying, soon to be fifty-nine-year-old woman, anyway."

"Baby." Toby put his hand on my knee. "You can still turn any man's head." He paused. "Have you noticed how Sid looks at you? Why haven't you set your sights on him. Have you noticed how much he looks like Richard Gere?"

If I were honest with myself, I'd confess that yes, I'd noticed. And yes, I had been attracted to him, but because of Nate, I never let myself think about Sid as anything other than a good friend. And now, with Toby and me, well, it just wasn't in the cards.

"I think I'm good with your killer blue eyes. Truth is, I still see the young man I married." I gave him a little push with my shoulder and wiggled my brownie.

"Besides, you have *skills*."

"I aim to please." Toby's grin turned serious. "Lex, I think it's time to talk."

"Yeah, I've been thinking the same thing." I wiped my fingers on a paper towel. "So, where do we go from here?"

"I know where I want to go."

"And that is?"

"I want to marry you, again." He laid his hand on mine. "Is that even possible?"

Honestly, I had been thinking about that very thing. I mean, why not? This would give Toby what he needed to leave this earth in peace, fully restored. And I did love him. Granted, it wasn't with the same passion as when we first married. But then, we weren't kids any longer. This felt right. As it always should have been.

"Yes, it is."

"Are you," his voice cracked, "serious? You'll remarry me?"

"Yes, Toby, I will."

He gazed at me and gently placed his hand under my chin. He stroked my lips with his thumb.

"I know men have said this before, but I mean it with every cell of my being. You've made me the happiest man on earth." He lowered his mouth on mine and kissed me slow and deep, taking me back to a time when all things were new and hopeful.

Yep, I truly had a bombshell to drop on the girls.

****

Mondays get a bad rap, especially this beautiful Monday morning. Today, for instance. First thing on my agenda, call an emergency Martini Monday. Second, hand in my resignation notice to Vince.

I wouldn't miss that guy one little bit.

Toby brought me coffee. "Here ya go." He kissed me, then said, "I'm going to check on Miss Cladie. Be back in a bit."

I smiled and nodded knowing it was probably her biscuits and chocolate gravy he was checking on. Before he left, he mentioned being our bartender for Martini Monday, but I told him I'd rather it be just me and my sister-friends and suggested he go to Sid's for the evening. He shrugged his shoulders and walked out the door.

I glanced at the clock. Finally, eight o'clock. I punched in Molly Kate's number.

"Hey Lex."

"Hey. The reason I called is because I want you to come over for Martini Monday tonight. I've got a big laugh just waiting and some good news."

"What? What's the news?"

I knew that would get her. Molly Kate would cancel her wedding to satisfy her curiosity. "Not telling. Be here at seven."

"I'll be there. What do you want me to bring?"

"Something heavy and sinful."

"How about a beer cheese fondue with shrimp dippers?"

"Perfect, and big cubes of sourdough bread too."

"Chocolate fondue and angel food cake dippers for dessert?"

"Yes, and I'll make my famous chocolate martinis to go with it.

"See you tonight, ladybug."

"Bye." One down, two to go. I called Avalee.

"Morning." A loud yawn assaulted my ears.

"What's got you up so early."

"Girl, get a real job. It's after eight."

Avalee yawned again, "Okay, so it is. What's up?"

"I'm calling an emergency Martini Monday tonight, seven o'clock. I have news."

"What?"

"Not telling. Is Ty back?"

"Yes, he got in a few days ago."

"Well tell him that Toby is going to Sid's. Maybe he would like to go too."

I heard her say something to Ty. Good lord. Both of them still in bed. "He says he'd like to go."

"Great. Molly Kate is bringing cheese fondue."

"How about me bringing some veggie dippers."

"If you must." That girl was always trying to be healthy, but we were wearing her down.

"Will do. See you at seven."

I checked the clock. Twenty minutes late to work already. Ha! I mentally counted the hours to Italy time. Almost three-thirty there, and Jema was probably home. I Facetimed her. In no time her pretty face flashed on my screen.

"Lexi! Ciao!"

"Hey girl. Listen, we are having a Martini Monday here at the house. Molly Kate and Avalee will be here. I have news. Big news. But seeing how our seven p.m. is your 2 a.m. you will have to wait until tomorrow. Will you be home?"

Jema's eyes went wide. "What?"

If anyone was more curious than Molly Kate, it would be Jema. "Not telling."

"Awww, come on. You know I hate waiting."

"Sorry, girlfriend. But get ready to smile, and just

laugh out loud."

Jema pushed out her bottom lip and frowned. "You hateful thing. I'm going to Zoom in anyway."

"At two a.m.?"

"I'll take a nap. I don't want to miss a Martini Monday."

"Yay! Love ya."

With a wink and a big smile, she kissed her fingertips and wave them, "Love you too. Bye bye."

I checked the clock. Eight-forty. Vince would be chewing his nails to the quick by now. And when I tell him about Nate, he'd start on his toes. Poor guy. I kinda felt sorry for him. To make amends, I might just have to give him Nate's personal number.

That would serve them both right.

****

I was exactly forty-nine and a half minutes late for work, so it didn't surprise me when I passed Vince's door and hear him bellow, "Lexi, come in here."

I poked my head in. "Yeess?"

He rose and walked around his desk. "Look, since you've been dating Nate, I've given you a lot of liberties, but—"

"—Nate and I broke up a long time ago." I swear the man turned pale. His jaw actually dropped. He stared at me in total shock.

"You did? Why? How am…"

"Yep, we did. As he so sweetly put it, *everything has a shelf life,* and I agree. Therefore," I reached in my purse and pulled out an envelope. "I'm resigning from the paper. I've written my column for this week and my column for next week stating it is the last one. I'll send them to you when I get to my office which I intend to clean out today."

Vince just stood there like a statue. I wouldn't doubt that, at any moment, he might just bawl his eyes out, because, you see, my breaking up with Nate meant he had as well. His man-crush was gone. Poof, just like that. I knew that despairing look wasn't about losing me.

He glared at the paper in his hands, glanced up at me, then turned and shut his office door. I felt sure once he read my letter and saw Nate's personal number at the bottom, he'd feel muuuch better.

I giggled out loud. I could still be a bad girl when I wanted.

That afternoon, Toby helped me straighten the house for my Martini Monday surprise. He seemed preoccupied and I wondered if he might be having second thoughts. We needed to talk—again.

"Hey, Toby. Let's get a glass of wine and talk for a minute."

"Good idea. I have something I want to say to you. Grab the cabernet and I'll be right back."

Okay, now I was nervous, and a little bit curious. When he returned, I handed him a glass and he gestured to the couch. We both sat.

Toby turned to face me. "Baby, I love you so much. I can't believe you are willing to give me a second chance." He contemplated me with his intense blue eyes. "But I have to say this. I'm feeling good now, but there will come a time in the near future that I won't. In fact, I'll become a burden. Are you sure you want to take this on? Take me on? I'll understand if you reconsider your answer."

Relief eased the tension in my body. "Yes, I'm

sure." I put my hand to his cheek. "Very sure. When I said 'I do' the first time, I meant it. And I mean it now."

"Well, if you are sure." He moved from the couch still holding my hand and balanced himself on one knee. From his pocket he took a small box and opened it. Inside was a delicate, white-gold, filigree ring with a sapphire setting.

"Lexi Lowe, will you remarry me?"

I grinned. "Yes."

He took my hand and slipped it on my finger.

"I chose this one because the sapphire symbolizes fidelity. Every day sitting in that prison I thought if only I had another chance, I'd never even look at another woman.

"But how…?"

"How could I afford it?"

I nodded never taking my gaze off the ring.

"Believe it or not, long before Claire, I had planned on taking you on that three-month tour of Europe we always talked about. I opened a secret bank account and put funds back for you to use as spending money. I planned on surprising you with the money and pamphlets from a travel agency on our anniversary. But instead, I just stomped on your heart. There was just enough in the account to purchase the ring." He kissed my hand. "I hope you like it."

"I love it, Tob. And not just because it is beautiful, but because you put so much thought into it."

He sat next to me, then pulled me onto his lap and brushed his lips across mine, then kissed down my neck and groaned. "I've dreamed about this."

This simple act took me aback. Honestly—and I know I sound stupid—but I hadn't thought about us being *physical.* I mean, he had cancer. Didn't that affect things? Well, now was the time to ask.

"Um, Tob, what about, well, can you…can we…you know…"

"Have sex?"

"Well, yeah."

"If what my body has been telling me these past few months, absolutely. At least for now."

I began unbuttoning his shirt. "Wanna give it a try?"

"Is the south hot in summer?

Indeed it is.

***

Needless to say, our little engagement celebration put me way behind. The girls would be arriving in an hour and I still didn't have the bar set up or the kitchen clean. While we lay in afterglow, we decided to marry as soon as possible at the Justice of the Peace. No big doings, just resuming life together after a years-long interruption.

I hoped I could contain myself and not blurt out my news to the girls as soon as they got here because I wanted to build up their curiosity until they couldn't stand it anymore.

Just as I finished straightening the kitchen, Molly Kate knocked on the door then headed right on in. Stan followed with a box carrying two fondue pots. "Hey, Lex. Where do you want these?"

"Just set them on the table. You just missed Toby. He went to Miss Cladie's. He and Ty are going to Sid's. You ought to go too."

"Sorry, but it's my night to mind the store and make sure our," he air-quoted with his fingers, "*ghost* makes an appearance."

"Huh?"

"I'll explain later." Molly Kate set her trays on the bar and kissed Stan's cheek. "Now skedaddle."

Just as he opened the door, Avalee stepped up on the porch with a large platter. He held it open for her. "Evening, Avalee."

"Hi, Stan. Hey, the boys haven't left yet for Sid's. You ought to join them."

"Can't, I have some haunting to do."

"Haunting?"

"Molly Kate will explain. Gotta run. Bye."

"Bye." Ava turned a quizzical look to Molly Kate.

MK pulled off her sweater. "Remember when we were planning Jema's wedding, you said something about how both you and Jema were proposed to in the library on the same night and I said I'd make something up about it having romantic powers? Then you said to make up a romantic legend, even a ghost? Well, that is exactly what we did."

"Oooh, tell us about it." I said as I carried a chilled bottle of vodka to the bar.

"Later. I've waited all day to hear what you have been keeping secret." Molly Kate set the fondue pot on the table I had set up for appetizers.

"First," I had my laptop set up in the living room. "We need to get Jema onboard."

"Jema?" Ava frowned. "It's the middle of the night there."

"I know, but she insisted." In no time Jema's excited face filled the screen. She held up a martini. "Hi y'all! Okay, Lex, what's up?"

"Now girls, don't get your panties in a twist. Fix

your plates while I pour."

"I don't know if I can eat until you tell us your news."

Somehow, Molly was still able to fill her plate. I loved it. They were already playing into my hands. "Why don't you start guessing? I bet you can't."

Avalee removed the foil off Miss Cladie's sausage-cheese balls. "Does it have anything to do with Nate?"

Perfect. I raised my brows as if to indicate that she was on the trail. "Umm, sorta."

Jema squealed. "I knew it. Y'all are back together."

I just grinned.

"I'd kick her fanny into next week if that's her news." Molly Kate plunged a shrimp into the cheese fondue. "I know, your column is finally syndicated."

"Nope, that won't be happening after today."

"Girl, did that panty-waist boss of yours fire you?" MK pointed her finger in my face. "He fired you because you broke up with Nate, didn't he?"

This was going better than I thought.

"No, he didn't fire me, but…" I shrugged my shoulders.

"Lex," Avalee looked at me with pleading eyes. "All this suspense has me tied up in knots. I'm dying here. What's your big news? Are you back with Nate? Are y'all getting married?"

I noticed the room got quiet. MK, Jema, and Ava stared at me.

"In a manner of speaking."

Avalee slapped her hands together. "I never thought he'd do it. Nathan Wolfe settling down."

Molly Kate dipped her chin and glared up at me. "Girl, have you lost your ever lovin' mind accepting that Yankee yay-hoo?

Jema choked on her martini. Ha! I had them right where I wanted them. I held up my glass and said, "Martini Monday is about to begin."

The girls held up theirs and said, "Here, here." Three sets of eyes lasered in on me like chickens on a grub. Molly Kate said, "Okay, if you value your life, you'd better start talking."

"Okay, first of all, I want y'all to know that I quit my job."

"Poor Vince," Molly Kate smirked. "Let him be your ring bearer."

"Well, that probably won't happen. Nate and I haven't gotten back together." I told them all about Miss Breathy Voice.

"I don't understand. I thought you hinted that you were getting married." Just then Avalee's glanced at my hand and saw my ring. She set her plate down. "No, you've got to be kidding."

Jema leaned toward the screen, "What? *What?*"

Molly Kate frowned. "Yeah…what?"

I couldn't stand it. My smile was so big my cheeks ached. "I'm engaged—" Purposeful pregnant pause. "—to Toby."

It was as if the earth stood still and then boom. Jema screamed and started dancing around. Avalee jumped up and grabbed me in a painful hug. "I can't believe this. Toby? When? How?"

Molly Kate put her hand over her heart and fell back on the sofa cushions. "Lord have mercy. Miracles do happen and Hell has frozen over."

After the pandemonium eased. I told them the whole story. Including that as of tonight, he would be moving back into our room.

"Sounds like y'all will be making up for lost time." Molly Kate grinned.

"For now, anyway." I shrugged. "There will come the day when he won't need a lover but a nurse."

Molly put her hand on my arm. "How do you feel about that?"

"Well, as Miss Cladie always says, 'Love gives no matter what the circumstances might be.'" My eyes grew warm. "I'm just thankful that we have what little time there is left together."

"Awww," Jema put her hand on the screen. "I wish I was there to hug you."

Molly Kate and Avalee drew me into a group hug. "You are not in this alone," said Avalee. "We are here to help."

"That's right." Jema nodded. "I will come home earlier if you need me to."

I placed my palm over Jema's on the screen. "I love you, girls."

After our hug, Avalee slapped her hands together. "Let's talk wedding plans."

I put my hands out. "No. None of that. We just want a simple ceremony at the JP's, really, I mean, there is absolutely nobody but y'all I'd want there."

"Then, at least let me make you a wedding supper at the B&B."

"That would be nice, MK. Thanks."

"And let me make you an honorary member of the Mile High Club. I'll send our jet to pick you up and it will take you anywhere you want to go for your honeymoon." Jema giggled. "You'll get that European trip after all."

"That would be nice, sweet Jema, but Toby can't leave the state."

"Well, shoot. Well then, y'all can fly to the Gulf Coast. How about that?"

"That sounds perfect. I'll have Toby make sure it's okay with his parole officer."

"And Ty can take pictures." Avalee did a little dance. "Oh this is the best news ever."

"Well, ladies. I'm going to sign off here and try to sleep." Jema blew a kiss. "I love y'all."

We blew kisses back. Then Molly Kate said, "How about a refill and fondue?"

"I'm all for that." I held out my glass. "Now, anyone else have good news?"

"I do." Avalee's smile was brilliant. "We found out Skye is having a girl and her name is Ava Elizabeth."

"Awwww, how wonderful." I nudged her with my elbow. "That child doesn't stand a chance."

"*And*, my grandma name is officially *Mimi.*"

"I love it!" I stuck my fork into a block of angel food cake and dunked it in chocolate.

Ava turned to Molly Kate. "And what's your good news?"

"That Lexi made her famous chocolate martinis. Let's have one."

This night was one I would savor for the rest of my life. Friends, laughter, bright tomorrows and, of course, yummy food.

Life was good.

****

Toby couldn't contain what he felt sure had to be the goofiest smile ever on a man's face. He tried to make conversation with Ty on the way to Sid's, but his mind and heart were so full of Lexi, it was hard to concentrate.

"Ok, Toby. What's up?" Ty grinned. "Do I have something hanging out of my nose?"

"No. Why?"

"You are staring at me and smiling like you just won the lottery."

"I did."

Ty glanced at him with a questioning look. "What?"

"Man, I gotta tell someone. Lexi and I…" Toby took a deep breath. "We're getting remarried."

"No kidding?" Ty hit the steering wheel with the palm of his hand. "Man, that's great. Congratulations."

"Thanks." Toby blew out a sigh and shook his head. "I never thought it was possible."

"I thought she was all gone over Nathan Wolfe."

"Me too. But she held back from committing. I blame myself for that. She just couldn't trust anyone after what I did."

Ty lifted his finger, "Or, she never stopped loving you."

"I know I never stopped loving her."

"Welp, we're here." Ty parked the car on the street.

Sid opened the door and called, "Come in guys. You are just in time to watch the Saints open a can of whoop-ass."

Ty held up a six-pack as they walked in. "Let's crack open one of these cold ones and toast our buddy Toby here."

"Sounds good." He took the beer Ty handed him. "What are we toasting?"

Toby couldn't hold it in any longer. "Lex and I are getting remarried."

The smile on Sid's face froze for a moment, then he held out his hand. "Congratulations."

The bewildered look on Sid's face wasn't missed by Toby. But he didn't blame him. This was the last thing he expected himself. It took Sid a few minutes to regain his composure, but soon they were all in the living room, bowls of popcorn on their laps, beers lifted in the air, cheering on the Saints.

****

After the guys left, Sid straightened up a bit and took out the trash. The air had a nip in it. He stared up at the stars in the night sky, sorting out the emotions battling within him. Lex was marrying Toby. He should be happy for their sakes. Only, at the moment, he wasn't—he was hurting. His budding romantic interest had been crushed like someone stepping on an emerging spring flower. The one time he dared to hope after years of loneliness. Honestly, he knew he'd been too guarded. After Barbara left, he focused on his boys. Then, when they were older and well-adjusted, he did date…a little. But the connection was never there. Just surface conversation. Until Lexi.

That woman was fire. Adventurous, inspiring, warm, and brave. She filled in all the places he was weak. All of the big plans he had for Moonlight would never have gotten off the ground if it hadn't been for her. She understood him. They were kindred spirits. He'd hoped their relationship would develop into something romantic and permanent. But now….

A dog howled from somewhere down the street. Sid looked in the direction of that mournful sound. "I hear ya, buddy."

He shook his head and went back inside. How selfish could one man be? After all, this marriage would accomplish so much. It was proof that Lexi had made the choice to forgive and love again. It freed Toby to live the rest of his life in peace and assured of her forgiveness. It was all good. All good—for them. And while that should've been enough for him, it wasn't. He knew he was being selfish, and he'd work it out.

But not tonight.

****

The girls and I had just finished cleaning up when Toby and Ty walked through the door.

Avalee rushed to Toby. "Congratulations, Tobman!" She wrapped him up in a hug and kissed his cheek. "What good news."

Molly Kate strode to him. "Amen to that." She gave him a bear hug. "Miracles do happen."

Toby grinned, "No truer words were ever spoken."

Stan knocked at the door. "My lady, your loyal subject is here to do thy bidding,"

Molly Kate handed him a box full of clean fondue pots and trays. "Tell him your news, Toby."

"Lexi and I are tying the knot…again. I got my miracle. My second chance."

"Congrats, man." He held up a box. "But don't let these ladies fool ya. They just need love-struck slaves to do their bidding."

Molly Kate slapped Stan's rear. "Oh get on with you."

Stan winked at her, "So I don't have to put my cabana-boy suit on when we get home?"

"Pssh. Honestly." Molly Kate waggled her

eyebrows, "But now that you mention it."

I opened the door for them. "Night y'all."

When everyone was gone, I turned off the porch light. "Whew, what a night."

"Have fun?"

"It was great. I had them going."

"We had a pretty good time too. They are a great bunch of guys."

"Did you tell them about us?" I handed him a glass of Shiraz.

"I did." He took my hand and led me to the den, that was once his room, but no more. "Let's sit in here and I'll build a fire."

"Sounds fabulous." I had to grin. Wait until the girls hear I actually used my fireplace. I nestled into the overstuffed sectional and watched him tepee kindling over the larger logs. "What did they say?"

"They thought it was great." He struck a match and threw it on the sticks. "Only…"

"Only?"

"Sid." The fire caught and soon crackled with heat. Toby sank down next to me. "He seemed kinda, well, taken aback at first."

"That's my fault, I guess. I've been so wrapped up in this convention center and boutique hotel we haven't talked about anything personal. I guess he was confused, seeing how Nate and I just recently broke up. I haven't spoken to him about *us.*" I sipped my wine. "He probably just figured that you and I had put our differences behind us and were on friendship terms."

"I can see why he looked so taken aback then. But, it didn't take long for him to be slapping my back, congratulating me."

The fire bathed the den in amber light. I wondered why I never used this room after Toby left. It was so comfortable. I laid my head on his shoulder. “Let’s set a date.”

“As far as I’m concerned, tomorrow would do.”

“That’s a little too fast. Besides, I need to check with Jema’s calendar.”

“Jema? Why?”

I walked my fingers up his chest. “Well, she has offered to give us a honeymoon, including her jet which will qualify us as members of the Mile High Club.”

“What’s the Mile High Club.”

“I sat up and looked at him. “Really?”

He shrugged his shoulders.

“The jet has a bedroom. With a bed. Forty-one-thousand feet in the air. In a bed…”

“Gotcha.” Toby swirled his wine. “You know I can’t leave the state, though.”

“How about Gulfport? The weather should still be pleasant. And we can stay as long as we like. Two, three weeks?”

“But where is the airport.”

“I hadn’t thought of that. They have a hanger in Memphis. Which is…well, shoot. I’ll call Jema tomorrow and see if we can fly out of somewhere in Mississippi. Levi can pull off some incredible moves.”

“Gulfport sounds great. The ocean, great seafood, long walks on the beach.” Toby pulled me closer.

The warmth of the room and the wine made me dreamy. I closed my eyes and listened to his breathing. It didn’t seem to me that he was breathing very deep and he was coughing more. The new pants he bought last summer were getting loose. I lost that dreamy mood and began to worry. Would it be a good idea to go on a prolonged trip?

"Babe?"

He kissed the top of my head. "Hmm?"

"What if I told you that I really didn't want to go away for our honeymoon?"

"I'd say you are lying."

I sat up. "No, really. Let's just keep this simple. Go to the JP, come home, and live like the old married couple we are."

He studied me, trying, I supposed, to see if I was serious.

"I mean, unless you really want to go?"

"Lex, I guess the only thing I'd miss would be the Mile High Club."

Leaning over, I nibbled his ear. "Baby, I can take you there right here in this room."

He took my wine glass and set it on the table. "You're on."

We made love by firelight. I was thankful for the dimly lit room because I didn't want him to see my tears. I was thankful we had what little time was left, but I was already missing him.

Chapter Twelve

I do…again

A few days later I rolled over to kiss Toby, but he wasn't there. I breathed deep the delightful aroma of coffee, meaning he was probably in the kitchen. Before getting out of bed, I checked the time. Eight o'clock. Slept in again. I was getting to be a regular lady of leisure. I slipped on my robe and padded to the kitchen.

Hmmm, no Toby.

By the coffee pot was a note that read, *Be back in a bit. Love you!*

Now where could he be at this hour? I poured the coffee and took a tentative sip. I hated old coffee. But this tasted fresh, he must have put it on a timer. He was getting really thoughtful in his old age.

I left the kitchen and shuffled to my office to check my email and a few of my favorite news sites. Lo and behold, there was a picture of Nate and Miss Breathy Voice posing for pictures at his event. Figures. She was young, tall, and voluptuous. The cameras loved her. Well, good for them. I didn't want to be in that position and didn't feel the least bit envious.

"Bye, Nate. Good luck." And with that I clicked over to check the weather.

After a couple of hours had passed I started to get a little concerned. Where was he? Just as I was about to call, I heard the door slam and Toby called, "Lex?"

"In here." I walked to the office door and he met me.

He kissed me on the nose and said, "Let's go get our marriage license, whaddya say?"

"Oookay, but what brought this on all of a sudden?"

"What sense is there in waiting?" He drew me close. "Let's get hitched."

"I just love it when you talk cowboy to me." I turned to leave when a thought occurred. I stopped and turned back around. "Where have you been?"

"My secret."

"Tell." I sounded like Molly Kate.

"Later. Now, what are you going to wear to the JP?"

"These jeans?" I spread my hands on either side of my body. "I mean, we've already done the fancy ceremony. This is just a refresher."

"I'd kinda like it if you dressed up a little, I mean, this is a special occasion. Wear that olive green dress of yours. It looks so pretty with your hair."

"That cocktail dress?"

"Yeah, the one that's off the shoulder. It looks really nice on you."

At first, I wondered when he had ever seen that dress, but then remembered I wore it to the Fall Fundraiser event for the homeless at the country club.

"Okay, but I'll feel kinda silly."

"Hey, it's our day and we will do it our way."

"What about you? What are you going to wear?"

"A suit."

"You don't have a suit."

"I do now."

So that explained where he had been. After getting dressed I strolled to the kitchen where Toby waited, and I had to admit, he looked pretty darned good in that suit, even though he was thinner than I had ever seen him.

"Well, let's go, handsome."

Toby beamed. "You're so beautiful. I can't believe we're getting remarried."

"Believe me, last summer, I would have said you were crazy to even hope." I wrapped my arms around him. "Neither of us expected this second chance at love. Let's make the most of it."

He crooked his arm and drew mine through his. "If you are waiting on me, little lady, then you're backing up. Let's go."

We got our license at the courthouse. Next stop, the JP on the second floor. I turned to go to the elevators, but Toby caught me by the arm. "Hey, before we go up, Molly Kate mentioned the other day that she'd like to be our witness. Let's go pick her up."

"We can't just barge in the shop and drag her out of there."

"She may not be at the shop, let's just run by her house and see."

"Well, at least let me call."

"Sure thing. Call while we are on our way. It's just a couple of blocks, right? And then we can all grab an early dinner."

This was all so silly. I felt sure the secretary would do fine for a witness, but Molly Kate would probably get her feelings hurt if I didn't at least ask. The phone rang once.

"Hello, sugar pie."

"Hey, Toby got a wild hair and decided we should get married today. Are you free to be our witness for a few minutes? We'll treat you to dinner."

"Of course I want to. Come on by."

"Okay, we'll be there is a sec, and I do mean a second. In fact, we are pulling onto the driveway now."

"Well, just come to the front door, I'll meet you there."

"Okay, bye."

Sure enough, I saw her walking through the solarium that joined her house to the mansion and before we could knock, she swung open the door. "Hi y'all. Come on in."

Something smelled heavenly. "What are you cooking?"

"Why, don't you remember?" She winked at Toby. "I did promise you a wedding feast. Stan has been busy all morning cooking up the best barbecue ribs in the south."

Now I was confused. She did offer, but we hadn't set a date when she offered said feast. Something was up. MK looked like she was about to bust.

"Hey," Toby turned to me. "Let's eat first and get married later."

"Wait. What?" I couldn't believe what I was hearing. "I got all dressed up and the JP's office will be closed by the time we finish eating."

"Someone need a JP?" Judge Weeks sauntered into the lobby. "I've been invited to this fine wedding feast. He clapped his hands and rubbed them together. "But first we need a wedding. So, let's get this show on the road."

Someone from the top of the stairs cried, “That’s what I’m talkin about.” Then Miss Cladie, Avalee, Ty, Jema, and Levi walked down the stairs. Stan joined Molly Kate and behind him came Sid.

Toby pulled me close, “Gotcha.”

For once in our long life together, he finally surprised me.

“Hey, Levi.” I rushed over to hug him. “Thank you for coming.”

“You look smashing, Lexi.” Turning to Toby, Levi stuck out his hand to shake. “Good to meet you, Toby.” He nodded toward me. “Are you sure you can handle this firecracker?”

“Good to finally meet you.” He laughed. “I’m going to try. I’ve had a few years practice.”

As usual, Molly Kate took the reins. “Let’s get on with this wedding. I’ve set up a spot in the parlor. Everyone go on in there.” MK took my arm. “*You* come with me and the girls.”

I followed them to a guest room upstairs. On the bed were three cream-colored dresses, a beautiful fall wedding bouquet with sunflowers, orange mums, and red roses. Next to the bouquet was a floral wreath made with tiny red rosebuds, miniature orange and yellow mums, what looked like laurel leaves, and baby’s breath. Swept up the side was a gorgeous pheasant feather and attached to the bottom was a veil.

Molly Kate shut the door. “We hoped Toby could convince you to wear that dress. But even if he hadn’t we chose these because they would go with anything.”

“You talked to Toby? How long has this been going on?”

Avalee laughed. “Four days? Sugar, we’ve been

racing around like greyhounds on a track."

I was at a loss for words. The only thing that would make it perfect would be if Avalee's best friend, Scott, from New York, could be here like he was for all the other girls' weddings. But this was such spontaneous decision and Avalee said he and his boyfriend broke up, so even if it had been planned in time for him to come, I imagine a wedding would be the last thing he'd want to attend. Still, I missed him.

After everyone slipped on their dresses, they went to work on me, refreshing my make-up and hair. Then crowning me with the wreath. It was stunning. I picked up the bouquet. "Avalee, you did a beautiful job on these flowers."

"Oh, I didn't do those." She appeared to be biting back a grin.

"Who did?" I knew Jema and MK didn't have any more talent in the design department than me."

Avalee gestured toward the door. "He did."

Scott stood in the doorway with his arms held open. "Giiiirrrrrllllll, you look fabulous!"

My hands went to mouth. "Scott!" I ran into his embrace. "Scott, you came. I can't believe this."

"Honey, you don't think I'd miss the last woman of Washington Avenue's wedding, do you?" He held me at arm's length. "Besides, this is a do-over with the same man…it gives me hope." Tears glistened in his eyes and my heart broke.

"Never give up hope, hon." I held him close in a tight hug. "If it worked out for me, it could work out for anybody."

He kissed the top of my head. "I'm holding on to that, thank you."

"Let's get this show on the road." Molly Kate led the way down the stairs to the parlor. Sid began strumming the Beatles tune, *And I Love Her,* and one by one the best women in the world glided down the aisle. Scott stood with me, crooked his arm, and said, "May I have the honor of walking you to the altar?"

"I would love that."

Toby stood waiting, drinking me in. I swear, I'd never felt more beautiful. Scott lifted my hand, kissed it, and placed it in Toby's.

Magical. That's the best way I could describe our wedding. It was nothing like our first wedding where our parents spent thousands of dollars. Our second ceremonial *I do* was not for show. It was for tell. It told of how love endures hardship, how fleeting life is, and the importance of savoring every moment of that life. This wisdom and the love of friends is what made our day so exquisite.

After the I do's were spoken, everyone went to work to get our wedding feast ready to serve. Toby and I escaped to the library to enjoy some *us* time and a glass of champagne.

We snuggled deep in the couch and watched the fire in the hearth. I sipped from my flute and let my gaze roam around the room while thinking back to when both Avalee and Jema were proposed to in this very room. I was happy to get my turn in this romantic setting.

Toby lifted his face and sniffed. "Do you smell that?"

I inhaled. "Pipe smoke?"

"And peppermint." He looked around. "I didn't smell it when we walked in."

"Me either." After a moment of thinking, I smiled. "Maybe it is Stan trying to fool us with his romantic ghost story. He sure has Molly Kate going."

"I haven't heard about that. What's the story?"

"Oh, they conjured up the idea of a romantic ghost story to add to the ambiance of the mansion. After all, doesn't every old house need a ghost?"

"Now I'm curious. How does pipe tobacco and peppermint figure into it?"

"I have no idea."

He sipped from his flute. "It's a nice combination. Reminds me of my grandfather. I wonder how he does it?"

"Again, no idea."

Jema stuck her head inside the doorway. "Time to eat."

"Good, I'm starving." Taking Toby by the hand I stood. "Let's go."

"Right behind you."

The table groaned under the weight of food. It was a feast for the eyes as well as my stomach. Barbecued ribs, fried chicken, mashed potatoes, roasted root veggies, Cladie Mae's purple hull peas, fried okra, and Molly Kate's Parker House rolls.

"Wow. I'm speechless." I turned and pointed my finger at Toby's nose. "Don't you say a word."

He lifted his hands in surrender. "All I was going to say was, someone give thanks fast!"

We all sat, Justice Weeks prayed, and then we all got down to serious fork lifting. When we couldn't eat another bite Molly Kate stood. "Okay, y'all. Follow me."

"I hope you have a blanket and pillow wherever we

are going because I need a nap." I hadn't been this food drunk since last Christmas.

We all obediently followed Molly Kate to the study. There, on a round pedestal table, was a beautiful three-tiered wedding cake. I felt my eyes warm and threaten to fill. These girls had gone all out.

"This is your favorite, Lex." Molly Kate handed me a knife with a ribbon tied on the handle. "Cut the first piece."

"Okay." I grinned up at Toby. "We might as well do this thing the traditional way."

Toby placed his hand over mine and we cut it together like we did at our first wedding. Lo and behold, it was carrot cake. My stomach begged, "Please, no." My mind said, "Oh hush up."

We each took a small piece, intertwined our arms, and fed—not smashed, mind you—each other. Moments later Jema pushed in a bar cart with filled champagne flutes. After we each took one, Avalee lifted hers. "And now a toast will be given by the one who knows all of us the best. My mom."

Miss Cladie cleared her throat and began. "In all of my eighty years, I've never witnessed a better example of love, acceptance, and forgiveness between two people. I've been blessed to see how you two were able to reach the point in this old fallen world to be able to accept each other's weaknesses, as well as your strengths, to finally come to the point of laying down bitterness and forgiving," Miss Cladie gazed at Toby, "Your being able to forgive Claire for lying," she turned to me, "and your being able to forgive Toby."

"By doing this you both freed yourselves, and once you were free, you rediscovered your love for each other. It doesn't always work out like this, but I'm so glad it did for you two."

Tears sparkled in Miss Cladie's eyes. "May the time you have together be full of joy and laughter, rich in love, and peace. I love you both."

Everyone lifted their glasses. Knowing the gravity of Miss Cladie's blessing, I promised myself that I would do everything in my power to fulfill that blessing.

****

Time spent with the dearest friends in the entire world, the best food ever cooked, and Toby beside me, would be what I'd cherish for the rest of my life. Now it was time to go home, so I started hugging everyone goodbye.

"Not so fast." Molly Kate left the parlor.

I couldn't imagine what else was on the agenda. Maybe she was bringing me the rest of the wedding cake, which is exactly what I didn't need. I was going to suggest she serve it with coffee to her guests.

She came back carrying an overnight case for each of us.

"What's this?" I looked to Toby, but he just shrugged his shoulders.

Jema grinned. "I promised you membership in the Mile High Club, didn't I? The limo is outside waiting to take you to the Memphis Airport. The jet is ready and waiting. You have a room at a sweet B & B in Gulfport, right on the water. There will be a driver waiting to take you there when you land."

Toby colored and he said in a low voice to Jema and Levi, "I never spoke to my parole officer. And I can't leave the state."

Levi clapped Toby on the back, “All handled, mate.”

Toby lowered his eyebrows. “How…?”

“Hey, no worries.” Levi smiled. “As I often say, ‘Don’t ask.’”

Toby pumped Levi’s hand. “This is unbelievable, thank you.”

I hugged both Jema and Levi. “This is amazing y’all. Thank you sooo much.”

Toby took the overnight bags and our friends followed us out of the house, throwing birdseed.

Scott pulled me aside and with an playful grin asked, “Want me to give Nate a message?”

I thought a moment, then said, “Yeah. Tell him *not everything* has a shelf life.”

He hugged me. “I don’t know what that means, but I’m sure he will. Love you, sweetie.”

“I love you too.”

He whispered in my ear, “Enjoy your ride.”

I frowned but he only winked.

Everything about the day and the wedding was perfect. I could hardly wait to see Toby’s reaction to the jet, and for our initiation to the *mile-high* club.

Chapter Thirteen

Honeymooners

Toby blew a low whistle when we slid into the limo. Champagne on ice and two flutes were at the ready. Soft Sinatra music played, and the lights were low. The driver's window was closed with a *Do Not Disturb* sign posted. So, this is what Scott was up to. Bless him.

I relaxed against Toby. Memories of my first trip to Memphis filled my mind. Only, this time, it wasn't to go to *someone else's* surprise wedding. It was my turn. A contented sigh escaped me.

"Man, this is unbelievable." He handed me a flute.

"Hon, you haven't seen anything yet." I kissed his neck. "Wait until we get to the Memphis airport. Levi's jet will make your jaw hurt."

He leaned over and nuzzled my ear. "Why?"

"From it dropping and hitting the floor over and over and over." I giggled. "Too bad the flight is only forty minutes long. We won't have much time to enjoy the *club.*"

"We can start right now." He ran his hands up my thigh. "Be all prepared."

"I always liked the boy scout in you."

By the time we reached the hanger, we were well prepared and ready to get into the air.

The pilot met us. “Good evening, and congratulations.”

Toby and I smiled at each other and I winked at him. “Thanks.”

He continued. “There are no stewards on this flight to Gulfport, as instructed by Mrs. Abrams. I have been told to give you complete privacy. Welcome aboard and please fasten your seatbelts until we are in the air.”

Toby lifted his eyebrow without taking his gaze off of me. “Just don’t take too long.”

The pilot laughed. “I hear you loud and clear.” He tipped his hat. “Again, congratulations.”

I watched Toby as he entered the jet. He scanned the cabin and took in the sectional sofa, the recliners, the big-screen television, and electric fireplace. He walked toward the recliner but I grabbed his hand.

“Not here.” He followed me to the bedroom where there was a love seat and the bed directly across. I patted the cushion. “Here.”

“Ahhhh.” He eased down, buckled his seatbelt, and snuggled me. “Now we can pick up where we left off.”

The fire we had stoked in the limo didn’t take any time to rekindle and as soon as the *all-clear* announcement was given over the intercom, we tore off our seatbelts and fell onto the bed. Our initiation to the *club* was well under way.

****

Toby held Lexi in his arms and watched her doze. This was all so surreal. Laying on a bed, in a jet, with his wife beside him. He savored the memory of their lovemaking—intimate and simmering. All too soon he felt the jet’s descent. Man, he hated disturbing her. But they probably needed to freshen up. He stroked her hair from her shoulder and kissed it.

"Hey, babe."

She stirred. "Is it time?"

"Afraid so."

Lexi sighed, stretched, and sat up. He ran his finger up and down her spine. "Thank you."

She rolled on top of him and kissed him. "For what?"

He pulled her close. "For a second chance."

"My pleasure, hon."

Over the speaker the captain said. "We will be touching down in ten minutes. Please fasten your seatbelts."

"Oops." Lexi lumbered off the bed and started pulling on her clothes. Toby did the same. They buckled in just as they felt the tires hit the runway.

Lexi shot a look at Toby. "How does my hair look?"

"Like you just had sex in a haystack."

"Oh lord." She finger-combed it and pulled it into a top knot. "Lucky for you, you don't have any."

"Hey," Toby smirked. "You don't have to be so ugly about it."

She bumped him with her elbow. "I kinda like your Yul Brenner look."

When it was announced they could deplane, Lexi glanced in the mirror, wiped off the smeared eyeliner and lipstick. "Oh, well. It's not like we are teenagers having sex in the backseat of a Ford. The pilot knows what went on."

Toby envisioned them making love in a car. "Hey, that's an idea."

She playfully popped him on the arm. "You men. I

declare."

To his credit, the pilot acted like nothing had happened.

A sedan waited for them on the tarmac. The driver tipped his hat. "Mr. And Mrs. Lowe?

"Yes." Toby wrapped his arm around Lexi, his wife. He still couldn't believe it.

The driver opened the door for them. "We will arrive at the Oceanside Bed and Breakfast in about twenty minutes."

In the car, Toby slouched against the seat. He felt unusually tired. Of course, it had been a full day. And then, there was the cancer. But he refused to give that last thought any real estate in his mind, today of all days. In fact, he'd suggest a moonlight walk along the beach. Sleep could come later.

Glancing out the window he watched buildings and palm trees rush by. Confusion set in. Where was he?

****

On the way to the B & B, I noticed Toby suddenly staring around in the car, as if totally confused. Then he turned to me. "Hey, Lex? Where are we going?"

Well, that was an odd question. "We're in Gulfport."

"Oh."

A few moments later, while the car was going seventy miles an hour, he opened the door and started to get out.

"Toby?" I reached over and pulled the door closed. Thank goodness he was belted in. "What are you doing?"

He looked at me confused. "I don't know?"

The driver swerved to the shoulder, slowed to a

stop, and looked at us in the rearview mirror. "Everything okay back there?"

I answered the driver. "We're fine. I don't think he shut the door all the way. No worries." Only I did worry.

Toby laid his head back and closed his eyes. Poor guy. He had to be exhausted. I decided we'd have something catered in for dinner.

"Here we are." The driver pulled onto the circular drive, got out of the car, and opened the door for us. I was immediately charmed by the light gray clapboard siding and the white trim. Just as Jema had said, it backed up to the ocean. The rhythmic sound of the waves and the taste of salt in the air invited me to hurry to the beach. It must have called to Toby too, because his energy revived.

A young man met us at the sedan and took our bags. "Mr. And Mrs. Lowe?"

I nodded.

"I'm Justin. Welcome to the Oceanside Bed and Breakfast. If you'll just follow me to your suite." We walked through the leaded glass door entry and into the foyer. The rich brown walnut floors gleamed. To our left was the staircase to the second floor, where, I assumed, our room would be. But he walked past the staircase and down the hall to the back of the inn. "You have the best room in the house, the Ocean View."

We strode into the living room and gasped. It had floor to ceiling windows across the back with a full view of the ocean. I looked closer to discover one that I thought was a window was actually a sliding glass door onto a veranda.

When Toby attempted to tip him, Justin waved him

off. "No sir, I've already been tipped." He grinned and arched an eyebrow. "Whoever got you this room, must really like you. My tip was more than three months' salary. If you need anything." He spread out his hands, "Anything at all. Just call."

After he left, we explored our suite. The inn's soft gray-and-white-trimmed color scheme continued inside the rooms. A navy-blue sectional faced a two-sided gas fireplace dividing the living room from the bedroom. Above the fireplace was a television. Toby studied the television a minute, then walked to it and pushed. It rotated to face the bedroom.

"Now that's just cool." He walked to the bedroom. "Lex, you gotta see this."

"In a minute." I wasn't interested in the television. The small hot tub in the alcove had my full attention. After a few minutes I watched Toby demo the rotating television and then I gazed around the bedroom. The king size bed had a fluffy, white comforter and a bazillion colorful pillows. I checked out the bathroom and fell in love with the claw-foot tub.

I turned to Toby, "I love it here. I wish we had decided to stay longer."

He quit playing with the television and smiled down at me. "Funny you should say that. I just got a text from Levi."

"What did he say?"

"He said that Jema told him that when we saw this place we would never want to leave, so he said for us to stay as long as we like."

"Wow." I walked to the patio door and opened it. The breeze had a chill in it. The hot tub would feel good.

He must have read my mind. "Let's take a short stroll and then maybe get in the hot tub?"

"That sounds amazing." I grabbed my sweater and Toby found his jacket. We stepped out onto the stone floor of the veranda. White wicker rockers faced a porch swing that was big enough to be a bed. A white iron and glass table with chairs were on the other side of the veranda. I decided this is where I'd have my morning coffee and my evening bourbon. Hanging baskets of ferns and pots filled with red geraniums adorned the patio.

We sauntered along the beach playing tag with the lacy edges of the waves slipping onto the shore. I faced the wind and savored the soft, saline breeze blowing through my hair. Except for Toby's little episode in the car, I felt at peace. He pulled me close, and we watched nature's masterpiece unfold. On the horizon the sun blazed yellow as it slipped behind the water's edge. Orange and red bled into the brilliant golden sky reflecting on each ripple of the midnight blue ocean. Both of us stood transfixed gazing at the beauty before us and Toby whispered, "I'm glad we are staying longer."

I squeezed his hand. "I am too."

Back in our room we were delighted to find a bottle of chilled Chardonnay, oysters on the half shell, shrimp cocktails, fruit, cheeses, and bread. Seeing this made me realize I was actually hungry again.

Toby poured a glass of wine and handed it to me, then filled his own and lifted it. "To us."

"To us."

Words I never in my wildest dreams thought we would ever utter to each other again in our lifetimes.

****

Even with all our great intentions to stay a month, after two weeks we were ready to go home and begin life as a married couple—again. Besides, Toby had another strange episode. He asked who was keeping our children. Later I asked him if he remembered opening the car door while speeding down the highway or asking about the children we never had. He didn't. So, I wanted to get him to the doctor as soon as possible.

We returned home just a few days before Thanksgiving, and we both looked forward to spending it with Miss Cladie. As her handyman—now turned manager of her floral business—Felix, always says, "She puts the big pot in the little un," meaning she went all out to make sure everyone at the table could eat their fill and enjoy every bite.

I anticipated having Toby with me for the holidays especially Christmas. All the years since our divorce, I'd felt like a third wheel at everyone else's celebrations. Sure, I enjoyed sharing these special moments with my friends, but after a couple hours, I started devising ways to escape the feel-good family gatherings and hide out in my empty house.

"Babe, our ride is here. Ready?"

"Yes." I kissed his cheek. "Let's go home."

The flight home was more sedate. We sat in the recliners and watched television while sipping a nice Pinot Grigio and munching on cheese and crackers. We napped in the limo all the way to Moonlight. I had to laugh. It was as if we had become the couple we were always meant to be and I liked it.

Chapter Fourteen

Gardening in the mind's soil.

Sid ran his fingers through his hair while attempting to study building plans, but intruding thoughts of Lexi made it impossible. He shoved back from his desk and walked to the window. She married a man, who just months ago she'd vowed she hated.

He wasn't sorry that she'd found release from years of animosity that held her prisoner. No, not at all. Still, her peace sacrificed his hopes—his imaginings—that maybe one day she might have considered him as a life partner. Then, just as he had dared to begin to hope, he witnessed a miraculous transformation in her and in her relationship to Toby.

He checked the clock. She was due in his office at eleven to go over their presentation to the council. He'd not spoken with her since the wedding and honestly, he didn't know if he could hide the conflict inside him. He plopped back into his chair and chided himself. *Lexi is a good friend. A very good friend. That's all. That is all it can be. It has to be enough.*

This didn't make him feel any better. He stood and paced the room, repeating his mantra. Then stopped when an epiphany struck him. He was making this all about him. Toby was dying for crying out loud. In the coming months she'd need his support and help.

If he loved her like he thought he did, he'd need to be there for her without expectations. And if Toby passed before the project was finished, it might be too much for her. If so, he would have to take up the slack and do it cheerfully.

His dilemma at this moment? Being objective and reining in his emotions.

****

After two weeks of lounging around in Gulfport, it felt good to be home. I was ready to get back to work. While we were at the Gulf, I got the greatest idea for our convention center and was excited to share it with Sid. Toby was glad to be home too. He wanted to get back into his routine of house husband.

Sadness clouded my thoughts. How long did he have? I shook my head. *No, don't think about that. Focus on your days together.*

I'd been thinking of ways to make the most of what was left of our time. The Christmas season would soon be upon us and I planned to fill it with beautiful moments. Toby and I would decorate to the point of being as gaudy as Miss Cladie. We would cook and eat all the sweet and fatty treats I could find in all my southern-approved cookbooks. Then, end each day watching sappy holiday movies, while snuggling and telling each other what we loved best about each other, remembering the good times we shared during our years together. And there *were* good times.

Buoyed by these thoughts, I finished dressing and prepared to leave for Sid's office. Toby stood at the stove cutting up veggies for his special chicken pot pie soup.

"Bye, sugar." I kissed him on the cheek. "Going to

a meeting with Sid to work on our presentation to the city council."

"Why don't you ask him over for dinner? We'll have plenty."

"Will do."

On the way to Sid's, I thought about how Toby and Sid had become such good friends. It was nice for Toby to have a man to talk to about whatever men talk about. I don't know what I would have done without my girls.

Sid looked up when I walked through his office door. A wave of his white hair slipped down over his brow. He brushed it back and peered at me over his reading glasses.

"You're ten minutes late." He gave me a mock glare with eyes the color of a clear morning sky and lids that suggested spending that morning in the bedroom.

Good grief, did I just think that? Yes, I actually thought bedroom. Hey, in my defense, while I may be a married woman, lord have mercy, that guy's handsome. Just because my hands are tied doesn't mean I'm blind. Even while dating Nate, I felt an attraction to Sid. I mean, he's the perfect package. Handsome, sensitive, and kind, and he dreams big dreams and makes them happen.

"You sound like Vince." I held up a tray of coffee and scones. "I brought a peace offering. And this time cinnamon scones."

"And just when I was starting to like lemon scones."

I slapped his arm. "You hateful thing."

There was that smile again. Broad with just a slight tug up one side. He gestured to the worktable on other side of the room. "Let's move over there. I've got some numbers for us."

I set the tray on the table. "Exactly where on the ouch-o-meter is the cost?"

"Somewhere between take me to the ER and intensive care."

"Uh, oh." I bit the corner off my pastry. "Old man Fleming will aim at us with both barrels."

"Well, a project like this isn't going to be cheap if it is done right. We just need to figure out possible financing before we present. I've got a call into several possible investors."

"How much?" I braced myself.

"Roughly, twenty-two million, give or take."

"Whoa."

"Yep." He leaned back in his chair with his hands behind his head. "Now on to more pleasant things. You texted to say you had a great idea for the convention center?"

"Well, after hearing those figures, I hate to suggest it."

"There's no charge for suggestions." He propped his feet on the table. "Shoot."

"Well, while we were in Gulfport, I hit upon an idea. I noticed how Toby was usually great in the mornings. Strong and raring to go, but in the evenings, he was washed out. Even though he attempted to keep it from me, I could tell. I tried to hide my worry, but the nagging in my gut was getting the best of me, you know?"

Sid's eyebrows drew together. He nodded as he sipped his coffee.

"So, while Toby watched television, I went for a walk on the beach. Sometimes I'd pause and just breathe in and out and focus on the moon's path along the water and the sound of the waves slapping onto the shore. By the time I got home, I felt at peace."

He bit into his scone and thought a minute. "Sounds like meditation."

I pointed my finger at him. "Exactly. I got to thinking about conferences and how tired you get after a long day. And while we can't bring the ocean in, I was thinking about a meditation room. We could put a huge aquarium in there, play soft music, have comfortable chairs, maybe even large pillows to sit on the floor. What do you think?"

"I like it. And it's unique, at least, I've not seen a room like that in all the centers I've been to, and I've been to a lot." He put his feet back on the floor and stood.

"Here." He tapped the plans. "This room on the third floor has a great view of the lake and it is pretty secluded away from the bar and patio."

"Yes, that's perfect."

We spent the next couple of hours sketching ideas for the meditation room and made plans for the big meeting where we would joust with old man Fleming. Just as I was leaving, I remembered Toby's invitation. "Oh, Toby said for you to come to supper tonight. He's making his famous chicken pot pie soup."

"Sounds great. Tell him I'll be there. What time?"

"Six?"

"Six it is. What can I bring?"

"Ummm, how about yourself."

"That I can do." He held the door open for me. "See you…y'all… tonight."

I waved and left. Smiling to myself, I looked

forward to an evening of relaxed conversation with both of my favorite men.

****

The aroma of roasting chicken and sage greeted me when I walked into the house. Toby stood by the stove with a dish towel thrown over his left shoulder. A habit I figured he'd picked up from Miss Cladie.

"Mmm, something smells divine." I gave him a peck on the cheek.

"Thanks, babe." He laid his spoon down, turned and brought me into a hug. "How did your meeting go."

I blew air from my cheeks. "Guess what this project is going to cost."

"I have no idea. In the millions?"

"Twenty-two, give or take."

"Wow." He hugged me again and laid his chin on the top of my head. "But if anyone can find a way, you can."

"I don't know about that, but thanks."

He stepped back to the stove. "Hey, did you ask Sid to come?"

"He'll be here around six."

After pulling the chicken out of the oven, he strolled back to me.

"I'm going to let the chicken cool before deboning it. Miss Cladie's making us a pan of biscuits for supper tonight, so I think I'll stroll on over." He winked. "I may stay for a chat and," he gave a grin, "snack on whatever she sets in front of me at her little table, too."

"Okay. I need to look over this multi-million-dollar price tag and find a way to soften the blow when we present to the council."

"Will old man Fleming be there?"

"Of course." I rolled my eyes heavenward. "That man has been on that council since the earth first cooled. Why people keep re-electing him is a mystery to me."

Toby took the towel from his shoulder and hung it neatly over the stove handle. "I suppose there needs to be a little salt to balance the mix."

"A little? Hmph. If that's the case, someone stumped their toe when adding him."

Toby laughed, gave me a soft kiss, then left for Cladie Mae's. I went to my office wondering how in the heck I could make a twenty-two-million-dollar budget palatable. I'm usually good at getting people to see things my way, but this was way beyond my pay grade.

While I paced around the room pretending to talk to the council, trying different approaches, my phone rang. Jema's name appeared on the screen.

"Hey, Jems. Did you get the pics I sent you from our amazing honeymoon?"

"I did. I'm so glad you liked it. That's why I called. I want to hear all about it."

"It was beyond amazing. In fact, I got really inspired for this project Sid and I are working on."

The conversation veered off topic, namely my honeymoon, and went straight to the project.

"Wow, Lex. That sounds fantastic. What a boon that will make to the town."

"Welll, it may not happen."

"Why, for heaven's sakes?"

"What usually kills the best laid plans?"

"Are you talking about that ornery Mr. Fleming?"

"Yep. When he hears the price tag, he'll go

ballistic. He might just have a heart attack."

"I'm not going to say it…" Jema chuckled.

"I know what you are thinking, you evil person. That could solve one hurdle." I sighed. "Only, there are also twenty-two million other hurdles."

Jema gave a low whistle. "He may not be the only one whose heart stops."

"I know. But there has to be a way and that's what I'm beating my head against the wall trying to figure out before the council meeting."

"You'll figure it out. Have you thought about investors?"

"Yes, I'm going through a list that Sid gave me. And I'm sure Toby will come up with suggestions. Some of his high-ranking patients are still fiercely loyal to him."

"How is Toby?"

"He is keeping up a good front. But I can tell he is struggling. His breathing is shallower, and he coughs more. In the mornings he feels good, but by the evening he's spent."

"Poor fellow."

"I know. And he feels bad for me. He worries about becoming a burden. So, he works extra hard and exhausts himself. I keep telling him to stop, that we have been given time to enjoy life together, but something in his *man DNA* just won't let him."

"That's tough on you, isn't it?"

"Tough isn't the word. I'm so sad for him—for us."

"Well, all you can do is let him set the pace."

"Yeah, lord knows I'm trying."

"Well, sugar, I've kept you too long. Get back to

your project."

"Okay, girlfriend. Thanks for calling. I miss you."

"Miss you too. Love you."

"Love you too. Bye."

After we hung up, I thought over my conversation with Jema. It was true. This time around, our relationship was very different. When we remarried, we didn't just pick up from where we left off. We entered into a whole new relationship. Instead of climbing the ladder of success, we enjoyed being relaxed and easy in each other's company. We savored the hours together. Physical intimacy was rare but our soul-intimacy was deep and rich.

I walked to the kitchen and poured a glass of chardonnay. Swirling the wine in my goblet, I sorta regretted taking on this project because it occupied too much space in my head. Time was fleeting and Toby had precious little of it. After a deep sip of my drink, I headed back to my office to resume banging my head against anything solid.

An hour had passed, fresh wine poured, and twelve emails to possible investors sent. Nothing. No ideas, epiphanies, or solutions crossed my brain or my computer. In the haze of my frustration, my phone rang. I answered and listened to the person on the other line, then dropped my glass, shattering it to pieces.

****

Toby sat, sipping coffee, and watching Miss Cladie cut the dough with the rim of a juice glass on her breadboard.

"I sure thank you, Miss Cladie, for making biscuits for our dinner tonight. I never seem to be able to get the hang of making them. Can't make dumplings either."

"Pshaw, nothing to it." Cladie grinned at him. "I'd be glad to teach you if you got a mind to."

"I might just do that."

She slid two pans of biscuits in the oven, then refilled their cups. "So, how is married, or should I say, *remarried* life?"

"To be frank, I'm still in awe that Lexi actually married me again." Toby drew in a breath and let it out. "It is the most amazing gift I've ever been given."

"And you are a gift to her, son. I haven't seen the true Lexi in years. She'd turned so hard. You've brought her back to us." Cladie sat across from him and laid her hand over his. "How are you feeling these days?"

He studied his cup before answering. "To be honest, I can feel my body changing." Glancing up he frowned. "But I don't want to say anything to Lex just yet."

"Why?"

"This will be our first Christmas together after years of being separated." He shook his head and let his gaze fall back to his cup. "And our last." Silence hovered like dense fog over them. Toby sighed. "Anyway, I want to make it special for her."

"Well, hon, anything I can do, just ask." She squeezed his hand. "Even though I've slowed down on my cooking, I still make way too much, and it'd be a mercy if you'd take some off my hands."

"That we can do."

The timer went off and she stood to take the biscuits from the oven. "I guess we'd better try one to see if they are fit'n to eat."

"By all means." Toby watched as Miss Cladie set

the butter dish and fig preserves on the table. "This may call for two biscuits."

"Eat the whole pan if you want, sugar. I made extra."

"No, I'd better just eat a couple. Sid is coming over for dinner. Would you like to join us?"

"Not tonight, dear. I guess you could say I have a routine and us old folks like to stay in our rut." She slathered butter and jam on a hot biscuit. "How's Sid doing?"

"Good." Toby lifted a soft biscuit dripping with butter and fig preserves to his mouth. He bit into the hot, fluffy bread and savored the marriage of creamy and sweet. "Miss Cladie? Speaking of Sid, I have a favor to ask."

"Sure, hon. I'll do anything I can."

The tiny mechanical yellow bird tweeted the hour from the Swiss chalet clock that hung on the wall above them. Toby gathered his thoughts while he waited for it to finish.

"What worries me is that I don't know how much time I have left."

"None of us do, sugar. Truth be known, we all live until we die."

"That's true, but my time has been put on the clock." He bent his head and rubbed his forehead. "I'm not afraid to die, but what I dread is leaving Lex again." When he looked up at Miss Cladie, his vision was distorted by tears. "I've been the cause of her suffering before, and I can't bear causing her to suffer again."

Miss Cladie's eyes glittered, and tears slid down her cheeks. "It's true. Great love leads to great pain and loss."

"I've been thinking about Sid."

"Sid?"

"Yeah. I have a feeling, well, more than a feeling, that he likes Lex. *Really* likes her." He wiped his eyes with his napkin. "I saw it in his face when I told him that Lex and I were getting remarried. Even before that day, I watched her with him while she was dating Nate. There was definitely an attraction, a connection, there."

"He's a good man. But what are you getting at?"

"I've thought this over a long time. After the new year, I'm going to plant an idea in both of their minds about pursuing a life together after I'm gone. Hopefully, if I'm right about his feelings for her, he will be there for her and hopefully she will develop feelings for him. And if that happens, I don't want either of them to think they are betraying my memory by loving each other. In fact, the thought of them being together gives me peace."

Pushing back from the table, Toby put his hands on his knees and looked deep into the old woman's kind eyes. "I have a favor to ask. After I'm gone, if Lexi ever talks to you about her attraction to Sid and her guilt about me, would you tell her about our conversation today?"

"Yes, honey. I promise."

Toby stood, relieved. "Thank you. I guess I'd better get back and finish up before Sid gets there."

Miss Cladie handed him a foil-wrapped pan. "Need some of my fig preserves?"

"Sounds really good."

She went to the pantry and pulled out a jar. "Here, I put these up last summer." She handed him the preserves and kissed his cheek. "Bye now."

"Bye." He leaned over and kissed her wrinkled cheek. "And thanks." He turned and walked home feeling stronger in his soul even if not in his body.

****

I guess Toby thought I'd lost my ever-lovin mind when he walked through the door and saw me jumping all over the living room waving my hands and laughing.

"Ooookay?" He set the biscuits on the kitchen counter and ambled over to me. "I give. What's up?"

"We have the money!" I grabbed him into a big hug.

"Wait. Back up. What money?"

"The twenty-two million for the project!" I sat on the couch and pulled him down beside me. "Levi and Jema are going to be our investors!"

"Whoa. That's fantastic. Why didn't you think of asking them in the first place?"

"I just couldn't. I know I always say it is nice to have rich friends. But there are boundaries, you know? I refuse to think of one of my dearest friends as a bank."

"I respect that. But they came through anyway, all on their own volition."

"I know! I can't wait for Sid to get here." I put my hand on Toby's arm. "Let's not say anything for a while and let him stew about it and then I'll pull out the champagne and we'll tell him the news."

"Yeah, let's build up the hopelessness of it all. And then bam! Problem solved." He frowned. "Do we have champagne?"

"No, I'll run get some." I jumped up then leaned over and kissed his cheek. "This will be such fun. Be right back."

I grabbed my purse and ran out the door to the car while imagining the look on Sid's face when we gave him the news. God love him, his dream for the town was finally coming true and I got to be a part of it.

If I say so myself, we made quite a team.

****

You know what they say about the best laid plans? Toby and I had the whole scenario played out in our minds. All through drinks and dinner we'd discuss possible investors and how to present to the council, especially Mr. Fleming. Then Toby would make it all sound so hopeless. Then I'd say something like, "Hey, enough of this downer talk." Then play like I was getting dessert. Toby would say something like, "I have the perfect drink to go with it." Then he'd follow me to the kitchen.

I wasn't sure if we'd be able to keep from giving the whole thing away by giggling under our breaths. We planned to return with a covered cake plate and champagne and glasses. By then, Sid would be totally confused. We'd tell him to lift the cake lid and underneath would be a note that said, *We have an investor!!!! All twenty-two million dollars promised for our project and more if needed! Courtesy of Levi and Jema Abrams!!!!*

Yes, we had it planned out to the letter. Just then the doorbell rang and Toby answered. When Sid stepped in, I couldn't help it. I ran to him, threw my arms around his neck, and shouted, "WE HAVE AN INVESTOR."

As I said, the best laid plans.

Toby put his hands on his hips and shook his head. But I saw that tiny curve of a smile. "How about a toast? I'll grab the champagne."

Sid's smile couldn't have gotten any wider. He pumped his fist in the air. "This is fantastic. Unbelievable."

Toby popped the cork and poured. "You should have seen Lex. She jumped around the house as if every step fell on hot lava."

"I had to do something with all that excitement." I raised my glass in a toast. "To the success of the tourism industry of Moonlight, Mississippi."

Sid added, "And to two of the best friends a man could have."

We clinked the rims and drank.

Sid set his glass down. "I hope you have a lot of soup. My appetite went from hungry to ravenous. Nothing like good news, right?"

"And for dessert, hot apple pie topped with ice cream."

Sid rubbed his hands together. "Ambrosia of the gods."

The soup was unusually good. Sid was right. Good news was a fantastic flavor addition. After dinner I suggested, "How about going to the den for our dessert. Toby's built a nice fire."

"Sounds good." Toby scooped ice cream on each piece of pie. We picked up our plates and I led the way. Toby and Sid talked while we ate. I preferred to indulge in my thoughts. I watched the yellow flames lick the wood and listened to the snaps that propelled glittery sparks against the grate.

After a while, I decided to clean up the kitchen.

"Well, guys," I stood. "I'll take those plates and do the dishes."

Sid started to stand. “Let me help.”

I pushed him back. “Nope. Toby cooks and I clean. And I think I’ll take Miss Cladie some of the left-over soup.”

“Okay, then.” Sid handed me his plate. “Tell Miss Cladie I’ll dream about those biscuits tonight.”

“She’ll love that.” I gave a little wave. “Be back in a bit.”

I grabbed a sweater. The night was chilly, but not winter chilly. That was the only thing that spoiled the night for me. Here we were in the first week of December and all I needed to wear was a sweater. That just wasn’t right.

But everything else—perfect.

****

Toby waited until he heard the front door close, then turned to Sid. “Good. I’m glad we have a few moments of privacy. I want to talk to you about Lexie. It’s really important and I don’t have long until she gets back from Cladie’s.”

Sid frowned. “Sure, what’s up?”

“Something is wrong with me, besides lung cancer. I’ve been having what Lex calls episodes. A few days ago, I went to see my doctor and he ordered a CT scan. It showed that my cancer has spread to my liver and brain. That means my life expectancy prognosis has been cut really short, really fast. I’ve reconciled myself to this, but what I’m not at peace with is knowing Lexi will be alone—again. And this brain cancer… I don’t know, but I think it’ll be tough on her. Really tough.”

“What did Lexi say when you told her?”

“I haven’t. She’s got enough worry on her plate.”

Sid pursed his lips and let his gaze fall to his hands.

Silence hovered for a moment.

Then Toby leaned forward and rested his arms on his knees. "Sid, I need you to be there for her when I'm gone. And I mean *really* be there for her. Be her friend, but not her brother. Are you following me?"

"Not really?"

"Look. While she was dating Nate, I thought you might have had feelings for her. But the night I told you we were remarrying; I knew for sure then."

Sid nodded his head. "It's true."

"And you still do, don't you?"

"Tob, I feel really weird confessing this to you right now. What are you getting at?"

"I just want to say, it's okay. In fact, you have my blessing. Sid, promise me that you will make her feel like the most beautiful woman ever born. Let her know how intelligent she is and how worthy of respect. Bring her flowers. Listen to her. Do all the things I wish I had time to do.

"Man, you don't know that. You may have years."

"No, if I live until spring, I will be beyond happy, but I have a feeling it won't be long now."

Sid shifted his weight on the couch and sighed. "This is a tough conversation. I don't know what to say."

"Say you will love her. You have my blessing. In fact, it will give me peace of mind."

"I can do all that and gladly. But, Toby, I can't make her love me."

"I know. Just be there for her and let's hope, no, let's pray for the best." Toby placed his hand on Sid's shoulder. "Deal?"

"Lexi is a special woman. What you ask isn't

hard." Sid met Toby's eyes. "I'll do all that you ask and as you say, pray for the best. But whatever she decides, I'll support her and be there for her."

"Thanks, Sid. That's all I can ask."

The fire popped sparks past the grate and onto the rug. Sid jumped up to stamp them out. Then flopped back on the couch. "Toby, I'm glad you got this second chance with Lex. I just want you to know that."

"This second chance, one that I had dreamed about but never believed possible, makes my next step in life easier to take."

The front door slammed, and Lexi called, "I'm back." She stuck her head in the doorway. "Coffee anyone?"

Sid stood. "Not for me. I'd better get back and revamp our presentation. Your great news changes everything."

Toby rose. "I'll have some with you after you finish in the kitchen. Meanwhile, I'll see Sid out."

Sid side-hugged Lexi. "Night, partner."

She kissed his cheek. "Night. See you tomorrow at the office."

Toby smiled. Maybe his hope would come to fruition after all.

Chapter Fifteen

All I want for Christmas is you

The morning of the town council meeting dawned bright, both outside and inside my soul. The dark dread of having to reveal the high price tag of our project no longer claimed my mind, thanks to Jema and Levi. While showering, I imagined old man Fleming charging in like a lion and after finding the project was all funded, being reduced to a lamb, no, a newborn kitten. I couldn't quit smiling.

The delightful fragrance of my favorite morning perfume—coffee—floated into my room and I followed my nose to the source.

"Morning, Toby." He looked up from his paper when I waltzed in the kitchen.

"Morning, sunshine." He lifted his face for a kiss. "You are mighty spry this morning."

I gave him a big smack on the lips. "Today is the council meeting." After pouring myself a cup of liquid gold I sat next to him. "I can't wait to give Fleming a full leash and then yank him back."

"I must say, you're evil, woman."

"Ain't I, though?" The coffee tasted unusually good. "I better get going. I want to arrive to the meeting early and make sure everything is in order for the more sensible, agreeable members of the council. I think they will be just as excited as we are." I rose and pecked Toby on the cheek. "Wish us luck."

"You don't need luck. Go get 'em, tiger."

Grinning, I scratched the air. "Rawr."

He chuckled, rattled his paper, and went back to reading. To any observer we probably looked as if we had never divorced. Funny how fast we fell back into that easy, comfortable pace. It felt nice to know I would return to my husband after work.

Now to battle.

****

The council meeting lasted just shy of an hour. And, as I'd hoped, it was successful. When all the hands had been shaken and the last council member left, Sid and I decided to celebrate our success by having an early lunch at the Mockingbird Moon Pub. It was a chilly afternoon, but the sun shown on the patio making it warm enough to eat outside. After ordering our beers and waiting for our burgers, we watched our little town do life. Shoppers strolled, delivery trucks rumbled down the street, kids played in the town square park.

"Just think. Sometime next year this town will be filled with tourists shopping and bringing business to all of our friends."

Sid lifted his beer. "To team Sid and Lexi." I clinked my mug against his. "To us."

Something, an emotion that I couldn't pinpoint, passed over his face. He took a deep drink and smiled. Foam covered his upper lip. I grinned and passed my finger over my mouth.

"What?"

"Are you thinking about growing a mustache?"

He frowned and then it dawned on him. "Oh."

I handed him a napkin and he wiped it off and smiled. "Better?"

"Much." I inclined my head and studied him. "You'd look good with a 'stach, though."

"Noted." He took another drink.

"Fleming didn't disappoint, did he?" The image of that man's smirk during our entire presentation still made me want to slap him into next year. Here Sid and I were talking about a conference center and a boutique hotel, something like this town had never seen or hoped to see, and there he sat, just like an old buzzard ready to proclaim our project as roadkill and pick it to pieces.

Sid laughed. "Nope. He sure didn't."

The man actually cleared his throat, stood, pushed his glasses up his nose and said, "Just how do you intend to raise twenty plus million dollars? Pull it out of your asses?" Then he looked around the room beaming over his little funny.

I leaned forward, relishing the memory. "If only I had a camera when you said, 'Actually, Mr. Fleming, I would do just that and so would Mrs. Lowe, if we had those kind of ass-ets. Sadly, we do not, so we will have to pull it out of the bank where our investor has already deposited the entire amount.'"

Sid snorted. "Fleming's neck must be on fire the way he whiplashed at that bit of information."

"And with his mouth hanging open like that, he could have caught flies."

Our giggles grew out of control. We were getting more than our share of stares, but we didn't care. Our laughter was cathartic.

"Hey, why don't we take the next couple of weeks

off?" Sid put his hand on mine sending warm currents up my arm. "Let's enjoy the holidays. Then, first thing January, get this show on the road."

"Sounds good." Thankfully our burgers arrived, and I pulled my hand from under his.

Sid didn't seem to notice anything, but I did, and it bothered me. How could I be feeling this? It wasn't right. I took a breath and tried to act normal.

"Got any plans for Christmas?" I took a bite of my burger.

"Cody and his girlfriend are coming over Christmas eve. Chris and his family will be with me Christmas day. You have anything planned?"

"Yes. We are going to share a real Christmas together."

Sid frowned.

"It's just that when Toby and I were first married, even though we did have some sweet celebrations together, after a few years we used the holiday as a way to impress colleagues and clients. We wasted so many years making it a business event for his practice rather than memories as a family. And then, after he went to prison, I just didn't have the heart to celebrate. So, I usually dropped in on Jema or Molly Kate. But this year I'm going all out." I bobbed my eyebrows up and down. "Miss Cladie style."

Sid grinned. "She sets some pretty high standards."

"I know, but I'm ready to meet the challenge. I want to create special moments for Tob and me." Those words caught in my throat. I swallowed. "Anyway, drop by and see my mess, okay?"

"I wouldn't miss the Washington Avenue Christmas competition for anything."

Oddly, I was hoping he'd say he'd come.

****

When I got home, I stood in the living room and looked around. It had been so long since I'd even thought about decorating for Christmas, I honestly didn't know where to start. Maybe music would put me in the spirit. I told Alexa to play Michael Buble's Christmas music and swayed as he crooned, *have yourself a merry little Christmas,* transporting me to holiday happiness.

"Ho, ho, ho." Toby sauntered from the den and joined me. He took my hand and we danced to the rest of the song. He spun me around and around, and said, "Hey, let's get a real tree this year."

I whirled back into his arms and looked up into his eyes. "Let's."

He smiled. "Grab your coat. It's actually getting cold outside."

"Good. I hate it when the weather is warm and sunny in December. There should be a universal law against it."

We took Whispering Pines Road to the tree lot on the eastern part of town. We walked among what seemed to be a thousand trees. The spicy scent of evergreen was absolutely delicious. Of course, we totally disagreed about which one we should get, but finally compromised on a Douglas fir. The tree stand guy wrapped it up and secured it to the roof of our car. I felt like I was in a Norman Rockwell painting.

On the way home, Toby asked, "Do we still have ornaments, or did those go into the trash along with everything that reminded you of me and my social climbing parties?"

"No, they are still packed away in the attic. I haven't decorated since we split."

"Leave them there, or better yet, give them away and get all new ones."

I had to admit, that sounded like a good plan. I didn't want anything to remind me of our painful past. A dark thought intruded on my mind. Next year, our new ones might be just as painful.

Toby glanced at me, his eyebrows drawn together, "What's wrong? Bad idea?"

"No, not at all. It's a great idea. I was just wondering what theme we should use."

"Let's go traditional. Red, gold, and silver. That just says Christmas to me."

"Me too." I thought a minute. "Let's decorate the outside with lights and yard art too. The neighbors will be wild with gratitude. For years they've been upset with me for being the only dark house on the street. They'll call it a Christmas miracle." All the decorating talk had taken me to another world, and I was aching to embrace it.

On the way home, I covertly texted Miss Cladie and asked if Felix and AJ would be available to help us with the tree. I knew Toby didn't have the strength, but he still had his pride. She texted back and said she'd send them our way. The moment we pulled in, both Felix and AJ just happened to be passing by.

"Need help with that?" Felix opened my door and helped me out.

"That would be wonderful." I winked in gratitude.

Toby held his hand out to AJ. "I don't think we've met. I'm Toby."

AJ shook his hand. "Glad to finally meet you,

neighbor." He indicated toward the tree. "Now let us give you a hand."

"Much obliged." Toby helped with the untying. Then the guys hefted the tree off the car and wrestled it through the door. Funny how a tree can look small on the lot and grow into gigantic proportions by the time it's set up in the living room.

After Felix and AJ got the tree up in the stand they stepped back. AJ took in a deep breath.

"Man. There's nothing that smells so good."

"How about something hot to drink, guys?" Toby gestured to the kitchen table. "Coffee? Spiced tea? Hot chocolate?"

"Nah, we'd better get back to Miss Cladie's. She's got us so busy with orders we don't know if we are coming or going." Felix patted my back. "Y'all take care now."

I gave each man a hug and opened the door for them. When I closed it, I turned around and noticed Toby quietly bracing himself on the kitchen island, struggling with his breathing. He did his best to keep me from noticing. But I did. This reinforced my determination to make our days together—our moments—unforgettable. The challenge was to keep him from seeing the worry on my face or hearing it in my voice.

"Hey, babe, why don't you rest a bit while I sort through the old decorations in the attic. We can drop them off at the shelter. I'm sure some families could use them. And then go shopping for new ones."

He didn't argue.

While he napped, I toted the boxes from the attic and loaded them in the car. He would have insisted on doing it himself and I couldn't bear hurting his ego. Just as I closed the trunk he joined me.

"I was going to do that."

"Thanks hon, but I didn't want to disturb you." Before he could respond, I grabbed his hand. "Let's go. And when we are done, I'm treating you to a hot chocolate at Molly's."

"Now that sounds like a plan." He helped me with my coat. "How about a slice of her coconut pie, too?"

"Deal!" Anything to fatten him up.

After we dropped off boxes at the shelter, we drove to the local hobby store and headed straight for the Christmas section. Toby and I stood in the midst of rows upon rows of garland, pine wreaths, ribbon, and colorful ornaments, smiling Santas, holly draped deer, twinkling lights in the fake trees, happy elves, and jaunty holiday songs. My spirit lifted and I closed my eyes letting the joy soak in.

"Pretty amazing, isn't it, babe?" I opened my eyes and met his gaze.

"Yeah. I haven't had Christmas decor therapy in years." Breathing deep the cinnamon scent from candles, I smiled. "I'd forgotten its enchantment."

He rubbed his hands together. "Well, let's load up."

Two hours later we had several baskets filled with ornaments, lights, garland, every kind of holiday bauble imaginable, lighted grazing deer for the outside as well as a waving Santa. I had no doubt that we would exceed even Miss Cladie's reputation for the most gaudily decorated house on the street.

"Babe?" Toby scratched his head and studied the back seat and trunk crammed full. "This is a lot of stuff.

We'll still be decorating on New Year's Day."

"You're right. I think we should call in the troops."

"Great idea. We can put on a spread." He slammed the trunk shut. "Ask Sid too."

"How about tomorrow night?" I knew that whatever plans our friends had, they'd drop them. "Does that give you time to get what you need to prepare food?"

"Plenty." Toby sat on the passenger side and stared off at nothing. Planning his menu, I supposed. Still, I'd tell everyone to bring something too. I knew Toby's limits even if he didn't.

Just as I thought, after we got home, I called everyone, and they all said they'd be happy to come and help. I mentally divvied up the work, the girls and I would work inside, and the guys could handle the outside, hanging lights and setting up the yard art. Then we could stuff ourselves like Santas on steroids, while enjoying the wonderland around us. My skin prickled with anticipation.

I was lost in thought when Toby snuck up behind me and slid his arms around my waist. He pressed against me and nuzzled my neck. "Hey."

I turned into his arms and gazed into his impossibly blue eyes. "Hey."

Bing Crosby's velvety voice sang "White Christmas," and Toby gathered me in his arms. We swayed to the music. When the song was over, he kissed me.

"I love you, Lexi."

I nuzzled against him. "I love you too, Tob."

"How about some naughty eggnog before bed?"

"Sounds wonderful."

"Do you want bourbon or rum in your nog?"

"Make mine bourbon."

Toby headed to the kitchen and I eased down on the couch and stared after him. Lately, and from now on, this was as naughty as we would get. But that was okay. Slow dancing to Bing was a great way to start the holidays.

****

The following afternoon, Toby put the finishing touches on his charcuterie board, perching the tiny elf he had purchased the day before, on top of the Gouda cheese wheel. He placed small snowmen forks beside the sliced salami, Havarti and Swiss cheese. A Christmas tree spreading knife lay next to the warm Brie. Red and green party pics held the prosciutto wrapped around cantaloupe slices. He especially liked the frosty effect of the sugared red grapes. A cut glass bowl held pickled veggies and tiny mozzarella balls. Thick slices of chewy bread lay next to small jars of orange marmalade and raspberry jam. All the board needed was some kind of fresh green flourish. He snapped his fingers. Rosemary. He strode to the patio and picked a branch off the potted bush. After washing it, he laid it on top of the unsliced part of Havarti. Perfect.

"Hey there." Lex sauntered in wearing tight jeans and an off the shoulder red sweater.

"You look amazing." He took her in his arms and breathed in the delicate fragrance she had splashed on. It reminded him of an herbal garden after a spring rain.

White Christmas played in the background. Bing's voice took Toby back to the evening before, slow dancing with her in his arms. Time was ticking away too fast.

****

Toby jealously guarded his charcuterie platter while I admired it.

"Come on, baby, just a taste," I begged.

He wagged his finger back and forth. "Nope. This feast is only for the eyes for the moment. But," he produced a small sampler plate, "do I know you or what?"

"Aww, thanks, babe."

"Knock, knock." Molly Kate breezed through the door followed by Stan who was loaded down with boxes. A very familiar sight.

"Hey Molly," Toby hugged her. "I said I was doing all the cooking."

She swiped the air. "Did you make fudge? Divinity? French dip sliders?

"Well, no."

"Hush up then, cos I did." She winked and swatted his arm. "It just wouldn't feel like a party to me if I didn't have a hand in the food."

"Merry Christmas everyone." Avalee strode in holding two bottles of wine. Ty trailed behind her helping Miss Cladie with one arm and holding a box with the other.

"Hey, y'all." Miss Cladie took the box from Ty. "Thanks, sugar."

"What's in the box, Cladie?" I put my hands together in prayer fashion. "Please tell me it is my favorite holiday snack."

She set the box on the kitchen island and pulled out a big bowl of boiled shrimp and then a bowl of cheese dip. "That I did!"

The doorbell rang and I opened it to see Felix, AJ, and little Junie. "Hey y'all, hurry on in."

Junie ran straight to Miss Cladie. AJ handed me two beautiful poinsettias.

"Grew these myself."

"Oh, they're beautiful." I kissed his cheek. "Thank you."

Felix handed me a small tree. The leaves looked vaguely familiar.

"Thank you, Felix, it's lovely."

He nodded me over to where he could speak to me privately. "Lexi, this here is an olive tree. It's a symbol of peace. Later on, when…well, you know…you'll need a place to go with your thoughts and grief. I hope you'll find the comfort you need by this here peace tree. I'll plant it anywhere you want come spring."

I couldn't stop my tears. "Thank you, Felix." I took the tree, set it on the table and hugged him. "You are one of the most wonderful men I know. What would Miss Cladie—all of us—do without you?"

He hugged me back. "I hope we never have to find that out anytime soon."

Molly Kate clapped her hands. "Okay, y'all. Let's get this sleigh sliding." She pointed to the boxes of lights. "Fellas, the ladders and staple guns are ready. Get to hanging and we'll do the same."

We all got to work. Bing, Frank, Sammy, Dean, and Nat filled the house with carols, while we decorated and laughed till our stomachs hurt. Junie helped Cladie Mae arrange the food, plates, utensils, and napkins. With so many helping the holiday decor was complete in no time. The guys came in stamping their feet and blowing into their hands.

"Man, it's cold out there." Toby stopped and looked around. "Wow, this is…it's dazzling."

I stood beside him and admired the enchantment that only Christmas could bring. The tree glittered with red and gold balls, gold ribbon, twinkling white lights, red winter berries, and tiny winter-white birds peeking from the branches here and there. Garlands draped the staircase and wreaths hung on the windows and doors. Frank Sinatra sang *I'll be Home for Christmas* in the background.

The perfect moment. That is, until MK's booming voice broke the spell. "All right everyone." she clapped her hands. "Let's eat."

We gathered around the buffet where Miss Cladie held her hands up. "Eggnog's ready. Now, who wants naughty and who wants nice?" Needless to say, we all held our hands up for naughty, just as she expected. Truth is, she didn't bother with making the nice since she knew little Junie preferred juice. Food, drink, music, laughter, and love of good friends—the elixir of life.

Christmas morning, I lay awake next to Toby, and listened to the soft rise and fall of his breathing. For weeks I had debated on a Christmas present for him. But what could I give? I mean, what do you give someone who only has a few months remaining? Nothing seemed right. And then it hit me, *You're a writer. Give him the gift of words.*

So, in the days leading up to Christmas, I jotted down things I wanted to say to him. Christmas Eve night I wrote my letter and printed it on Christmassy paper, sealed it and stuck it in the tree and hoped it gave him all that he needed for his remaining time.

Toby rolled on his side and pulled me to him in spoon-fashion. “Merry Christmas.”

“Merry Christmas, baby.” Rising up on my elbow, I turned to him. “Coffee?”

“Please.” He flopped over on his back. “Just give me a minute to wake up.”

“I can bring it to you.”

“No,” he rubbed his eyes. “I’ll be along in a bit.”

I waited for him in the den where I had a fire going. Ten minutes passed, then twenty minutes. Something told me I had better check on him. I poked my head in the bedroom, but he wasn’t in bed, nor in the bathroom. Where had he gone? Frantically, I called out to him, but no answer. I strode through the living room and saw him through the window standing in the yard, in his shorts and tee shirt. He looked confused.

“Toby?” I ran outside. “Why are you outside? It is freezing out here.”

His expression stayed blank as he looked about him.

I took his hand. “Let’s go back in and warm you up.”

When he tried to follow me, I noticed him staggering. I reached for his left hand, but it was limp. “Baby? Do I need to get Ty to help you inside?”

Then, as if a lightbulb went on, he frowned and asked, “Why are we outside? It’s freezing out here.” Then he looked down. “Good lord. I’m in my underwear.”

I reached for him again. “Let’s get inside.”

He limped in after me, complaining of pain on his left side. Clearly, something was going on and it had me worried. I got his robe, poured his coffee, and led him into the den to warm up in front of the fire. After a few sips, he said, "Well, that was weird."

"What happened, babe?"

"I don't know. I got up to join you and the next thing I know you are with me in the yard."

For a long time, we stared at the flames dancing over the wood and bursting into sparks. He broke the silence.

"Actually, I do know." He took my hand. "I've known for several weeks now, but didn't want to spoil the holidays."

"What?"

"After we got home from Gulfport, I went to the doctor and told him about my *episodes.* Baby, it turns out I also have metastatic brain cancer."

My hand went to my mouth. "Oh, no."

"I didn't want to tell you, but seeing how these," he let go of my hand and made air quotes, "episodes keep happening, I think you should know."

Words wouldn't come. All I could do was stare at him.

He held up his finger. "Hey, I got you something. Wait here." He stood and left the room.

I almost stopped him. There was no telling where he'd end up. But soon he returned with a small envelope trimmed with gold filigree. "Merry Christmas."

"Thank you, sweetheart." I expected a sweet letter and slipped my finger beneath the seal and he went on to explain.

"I had one friend left after the whole adultery fiasco happened and he happened to be my financial advisor. So, when it looked like I was heading to prison, I made him my power of attorney and he continued to pay my life insurance policy. I kept you as my beneficiary. It was, after all, the least that I could do, and I increased the value to one and a half million dollars."

I stared at the paperwork through the film of tears.

He put his hand on mine. "I know it isn't very romantic. But I wanted to be sure you were financially taken care of."

"Thank you, baby." Then I brushed my tears away. "It means everything to me that you are protecting my future."

He smiled. "That means everything to me too."

I took his hand. "Come with me to the living room. Your present is in there."

The morning was overcast, which gave our living room a fairy-like glow from the white lights on the tree. He sat in his recliner and watched me pull the envelope from the tree branches, then I lowered on the arm of his chair. "This gift is from my heart. I'm going to make breakfast and leave you alone to read it."

I kissed his cheek and left.

****

Toby watched Lexi leave the room, then examined the envelope. He really didn't expect anything. After all, what do you give a dying man? Still, his amazing wife had thought of something. He eased the snowflake bordered paper from the envelope and began to read.

Dear Toby,

I read a quote that said we are chained to what we do not forgive. Sadly, I'm proof of the truth this quote states. I have lived too many years chained—imprisoned—by my own willful stubbornness. Just like

Scrooge in A Christmas Carol, *I forged the chain of hate link by link and as Marley said in the story, it was a ponderous chain.*

Fate used you to set me free. But it pains me to know that my freedom came at the costliest of prices—your life—and that doesn't seem fair. Avalee once said, "Life is truly strange—both unfair and beyond generous." I have no idea what I've done to deserve such generosity. Your humility and patience opened my eyes and heart. These past few months have been the best of my life. I am free, totally free. When the past comes to my mind, it no longer hurts. I have, as it is said, closed the door to pain and regret. As a matter of fact, I want to be like you in so many ways. Because of you, I've learned patience in the face of adversity. When it is time for you to move on from this earth, go in peace. I will miss you, but because of you I am strong. You will always be in my heart and remembered as my great love.

He swiped tears from his eyes, then read the letter again. This was the best gift he had ever received. However, he didn't want to be remembered as her *only* great love. God willing, he had enough time to plant a seed in her heart that would one day bloom into an even greater love.

Chapter Sixteen

Our long goodbye

The day after Christmas, I could tell Toby felt bad. If breathing wasn't hard enough, he had also been suffering these cognitive fluctuations. We decided to schedule hospice to come the first week of January. Looking at him now, so tired and often in pain, I wished I'd scheduled them earlier.

"Hey, babe."

I turned to my smiling husband. "Hey."

"I was thinking about inviting Sid over to help us with all our leftovers."

"Good idea." Over the holidays Toby had cooked like he wanted to cram the next twenty-five Christmas dinners into one. "Are you going to call, or do you want me to?"

"I'll call." His smile didn't reach his eyes. A little frown grew deep between his brows.

"Are you sure? Do you feel okay?"

"Yeah, just a bit of a headache. I'll be fine."

Toby called, and by the sound of the one-sided conversation I overheard, Sid had accepted. I headed to the kitchen to start pulling out leftovers to reheat.

"He said he was on his way." Toby grinned. "Typical bachelor. What he needs is the love and care of a good woman. Maybe next time around."

That was true. Sid was a fine man who deserved more than what he had the first time. Still, two good sons came from that disastrous union. He was so handsome back then and still is now. His ex was crazy. He would have been on my radar for sure if this thing with Toby hadn't happened. Especially since my relationship with Nate had apparently hit the expiration date.

My phone rang, breaking into my thoughts. The screen read *Nate.* Well, now, speak of the devil. Why was it that almost every time he crossed my mind, he called? Surely we don't have that kind of soul connection. I debated whether to answer it or not. My thumb finally decided by hitting decline. Little Miss Breathy Voice's shelf-life must have expired too. At least I lasted a couple of years.

A voicemail alert popped up. Curious, I listened.

"Hey, Red. Umm, yeah, hey, listen. I'm passing through close to you in early June on my way to speak at a convention and wondered if we could meet for drinks? I want to clear something up with you about our last conversation. I'd appreciate you giving me a call."

Clear something up? What on earth did he have to say? Oh well, I had too much on my plate to waste time with him. I deleted the message. "Sorry Nate. Consider yourself expired."

"What's that, hon?"

I whirled around. Had Toby heard me say Nate? "Telemarketer."

"I thought you were on the Do Not Call list."

"I am, but somehow they get through." Thank goodness he hadn't heard. The last thing he needed was to worry about me and Nate, who was way off my radar.

Sid arrived just as I closed the doors on double ovens that were crammed with leftovers. "Hey, Sid. Dinner will be ready in about thirty minutes. How 'bout a drink?"

"Sounds great. Where's Tob?"

I looked around. "I'm not sure. Make yourself something and I'll check."

Sid walked to the bar and I checked in our room. He wasn't there. I tried to not panic, so I walked back into the living room. Sid had just made a bourbon and seltzer. "Find him?"

"No, let me check in the den."

He set his drink down. Sid knew I was worried. "I'll check upstairs."

I didn't find him in the back and a growing panic gnawed in my stomach.

From upstairs Sid's voice boomed out. "Lexi. Quick. Upstairs."

"What the?" I flew up the steps and found Sid holding onto Toby by the waist. Toby was half-way out the guestroom window and fighting Sid.

"Let go, I just want to take a walk on the balcony."

"Baby. This is Lexi. Honey. There is no balcony."

Toby turned to my voice and looked at me with empty eyes, that slowly filled with recognition. "Lex?" He looked at Sid then at his leg hanging out the window. "Not again?"

He let us help him back inside, then he collapsed on the floor. "God. Ya'll, I'm so sorry." Scrubbing his face with his shaking hands, he blew out a breath. "I can't do this to you, Lexi."

"Do what, hon?"

"These crazy things."

I kneeled beside him. "Don't say that. Every day we have left is precious. I'll just have to keep a closer eye on you."

"But that isn't a life for you. It is a prison."

Sid put his hand on Toby's shoulder. "Hey, bud, she isn't alone in this. I'm here for you too."

Toby stared up at me, then Sid. "Man." His gaze fell to his lap. "I don't deserve you two."

Sid helped Toby up. "Hey, remember that song, 'He ain't Heavy, He's My Brother'?"

"Yeah."

Sid put his hand on Toby's shoulder. "Remember the line about being strong enough to carry him? Well, that's the way I feel. I'm here for you, buddy." Sid smiled. "And the way that dinner is smelling, I'm ready to carry you on my shoulders downstairs to the kitchen. I'm hungry as a wolf. Let's eat."

I followed the guys down the stairs. Toby turned back to being his gregarious self, talking to Sid over drinks while I pulled dinner out of the stoves and set the table. I hoped they'd eat a lot because I had lost my appetite.

****

New Year's Eve came and passed like any other day. Dawn peeked through the curtain making a patchwork of shadows on the bed. I stared in the dark at Toby's silhouette next to me. It was the first day of the year and honestly, I couldn't celebrate what this new year promised to bring.

Toby stirred, then rolled over and faced me. "Morning. Happy New Year."

"Happy?" I couldn't wrap my head around this

new year's greeting that I'd rattled off for the past five decades of my life. "You are dying. I'm losing you again." Warm tears filled my eyes and slid down my cheek.

"Hey. Babe." He tenderly thumbed the dampness off my face. "We are all going to die. The only difference is I've been given a time frame."

When I didn't answer he scooted close and nuzzled my neck. "Hey, I want you to promise me something."

"What?"

"Don't give up on love. Marry again."

"I can't think about that right now."

He hugged me tighter. "I know. But it's *all* I can think about. I want to, no, I need to know that you will finish out your days with someone who appreciates the amazing woman you are. And…"

He didn't finish his sentence, so I turned over and searched his eyes. "And what?"

"And that person isn't Nate."

"What do you mean?"

"I heard."

"Then you must have heard me say he was expired."

"Yes. But I also know he's a determined man. I don't feel good about him."

I kissed Toby's forehead. "Then who do you feel good about?"

"I'm not saying. But you will know. In time."

"Toby, I promise to try and give love another chance."

He sighed and smiled. "Thank you, baby. You've given me the release I need."

Sitting up, I swung my legs over the edge of the

bed. "All I know is that I need coffee. Want me to bring you some?"

"No, I'm getting up."

He grimaced when he leaned on his left side.

"You need help?"

"No, babe. Thanks, though."

I put on my robe and slippers. The minutes we had together were sifting through life's hourglass. I wish I had a way to slow them down.

****

It seemed to me that once I promised Toby I'd give love another chance, he made up his mind that he was ready to go. In the two weeks since our conversation on New Year's morning, he had disappeared a little each day. Hospice said this was normal. I had a hospital bed set up in our room which made caring for him easier on both of us. I'd sit beside him for hours and watch every breath, not wanting to miss his last. Then, one morning it was as if the clouds of his mind cleared, he looked at me and smiled. I raised the head of his bed and we talked. He told me how grateful he was for me and how much he loved me. We talked for an hour. It was like nothing was wrong. Like he wasn't sick at all. But just as the clouds had parted, they soon gathered back together. Before he closed his eyes, he mumbled, "Remember, give love another chance."

He never woke again.

Two mornings later, on January 17th, I kept my vigil watching the rise and fall of his chest. I wanted coffee, so just in case he happened to open his eyes and see I wasn't there, I leaned close and whispered, "Tob, I'm going to make a cup of coffee. I'll be right back."

When I returned, he was gone.

Tears coursed down my face as I lifted his hand to my lips and then held it. Even though I felt relieved that his suffering was over, I still battled the widening gulf of loneliness inside me. Still holding his hand, I called Hospice. Then I called my girls. Within minutes, Miss Cladie, Avalee, and Molly Kate were by my side embracing me while saying their goodbyes to Toby. I remained by his side while Miss Cladie and Molly Kate bustled around in the kitchen. Avalee sat beside me saying nothing. Her presence was all I wanted or needed. After a few minutes, the fragrance of coffee drifted into the living room. So strange how that comforted me. Soon, the house would be filled with those paying their respects. Thank goodness for Cladie Mae, and Molly Kate. They would be the perfect hostesses. I couldn't face anyone or anything.

After the funeral home left with Toby's body, I trudged into my bathroom. His robe hung by the shower and I buried my face in it. Everything was just as he left it. Like he was in the kitchen cooking breakfast. I could almost hear him clanging pans.

I thought back to him asking me to love again. It was his dying wish. But I didn't know if I could keep my promise.

****

Toby's service was just as he had requested. Small, a lot of food and friends. Jema had flown in and planned on staying with me as long as I needed her. She would never know the comfort this gave me.

When everyone had left, the girls and Miss Cladie stayed behind to clean up, bless them. They wouldn't let me do a thing.

"Here, hon." Jema handed me a mug of hot tea.

"Sugar, while I'm here, I plan on making a pest of myself unless you'd rather be left alone."

"Please. Stay close." I took a sip of tea, then asked, "Would you ask Miss Cladie to come here for a moment?"

"Sure, hon." Moments later, Cladie Mae walked into the living room, followed by Avalee and Molly Kate.

"Miss Cladie, I have a favor to ask."

"What is it, sugar?"

"Toby asked me to scatter his ashes in a field so they could catch in the wind. He liked the idea of freedom this gave him. I've been thinking of places where I could do this. I thought of the lake or my back yard under the tree he loved so much. Then the perfect place came to my mind. Your land where the Moonlight Market meets every Saturday in the summer. There in that big field where the wildflowers bloom each spring? Would it be okay with you for me to scatter them there?"

"Of course, baby girl." Miss Cladie sat beside me on the couch and put her arm around my shoulders and squeezed me to her.

Avalee sat on my other side. "I think that's the perfect place."

Molly Kate wiped her eyes with the hem of her apron. "Me too."

Two weeks later, Toby's remains were delivered. It felt so strange holding that box. It held what used to be my husband. I couldn't wrap my mind around this. Fresh pain electrified my body and I missed him more than ever. I crumpled to the floor, hugging it to my chest.

"Lexi, honey, what's wrong." Jema kneeled beside me and I showed her the carton. She wrapped me in her arms and rocked me like a child. No words were spoken. None were needed.

When I gathered myself, I stood. "I'm taking him to the field now."

"Do you want me to come with you?"

"No, I'll be fine. I think I need to do this alone."

"I'll be here when you get back with a glass of wine."

I hugged her, slipped on a coat, and left.

I was half-way there when my phone rang. It was Miss Cladie.

"Hello."

"Hey, ladybug. Jema called to let me know Toby's remains arrived and that you are on your way to scatter them. Listen, go to the small copse of trees by the duck pond. Toby loved it there."

"He did? I didn't know that."

"Yes, he went there to pray and meditate when he felt overwhelmed." Her voice cracked "I think he'd love you releasing his ashes there."

"Thank you, Miss Cladie. I'll walk that way now."

"Take your time but let us know when you are on your way back."

"I will." I disconnected the call and continued my walk to Toby's final resting place.

When I reached the duck pond, I was surprised to find a beautiful iron memorial bench. Toby's name had been laser cut on the backrest. I ran my hand over it and sighed. Miss Cladie's doings, no doubt. God love her.

I eased on the bench and set the box beside me. It was a cloudy day, fitting for my mood. A chilly breeze blew at my back. I hugged my coat tighter. The ducks were impervious to the chill. They floated and bobbed, never paying attention to me. Somewhere I heard a cardinal, *cheer, cheer, cheer, birdie, birdie, birdie.*

Lifting my face to the billowing clouds I released the breath I'd been holding and closed my eyes and focused on feeling of the moment, the birdsong, and the wind in the trees. Peace filled me.

It was time. I stood and walked to the middle of the field, opened the box, and let the wind take Toby's remains far and wide.

"Goodbye, my love."

No sooner had the words left my mouth, a beam of sunlight broke through the clouds. I let it bathe my upturned face, feeling that Toby was letting me know he was at peace too.

Chapter Seventeen

Keeping a promise

Sid cast a concerned glance across the room where Lexi studied fabric swatches. The projects were going well, in fact, they were ahead of schedule. In the four months since Toby's death, she had thrown herself into the projects and worked long hours into the night. When he mentioned that she should slow down, take it easy, she said working like this helped her. But had it? She had grown thin and fatigued.

Their relationship suffered too. Their camaraderie dwindled to project details. She didn't have the emotional energy to do much else. She'd lost her verve, which, of course is understandable. But he, like Molly Kate, worried that she was moving from grief into despair.

He had to do something, after all, he promised Toby he'd take care of her. But how?

"Hey, Lex."

She lifted her eyes from the swatches to him. "Uh huh?"

"Let's go to the site and then grab a bite to eat."

"I'm not really hungry."

"Well, I am, and you can at least attempt to eat."

Ignoring him, she held up two swatches. "Which of these do you like for the couches and chairs in the hotel?"

Sid walked over and he contemplated the soft saddle-brown leather. "This one. It'd be easier to keep clean."

She studied the materials. "You have a point, but I like the color and texture of this one." She pointed to the terracotta herringbone swatch.

"I like that too." He thought a minute. "Could we somehow combine them?"

"Well," she laid the fabric over the leather. "the places that get stained or dirty are the arm rests and cushions. So, we could have the arm rests and cushions made of leather and the backrest and sides made of fabric. "And…" She took complimenting fabric colors of sand, clay, and burnt orange. "We can have pillows made from these."

Sid nodded. "It fits the industrial vibe, and still looks elegant at the same time." Laying his hand on her shoulder he gave her a light squeeze. "Great taste, my lady."

He hoped she would remember their banter about his being a knight when this project was just an exciting idea.

She paused, then dropped her head. "That seems like a life-time ago."

He pulled up a chair beside her. "It was." Taking her hand in his, he rubbed his thumb over her smooth flesh. "Hey. I made a promise to my friend. Please make it easier for me to keep it."

She glanced up at him and frowned. "What do you mean?"

"Toby asked me to take care of you. And I feel I've failed him these past four months. You are working yourself to death. You stay late and come in early. You are burning the candle at both ends. I'm worried about you."

"You haven't failed him. Work keeps my mind off…things. I hate going to the house now. It's so empty.

Lexi dropped her gaze and shook her head. "It's all so bizarre. I lived alone for years. Then Toby moves in, lives there only six months, and now it feels like a tomb."

This gave him an idea. He took her other hand in his. "Look, I don't want to pressure you, but I'd like to bring dinner to your house. We can have a glass of wine, toast Toby, and remember him."

She opened her mouth, closed it, then nodded her head. "Okay."

He couldn't believe she'd agreed and wanted to pull her into a jubilant hug. But knowing that wouldn't be a good idea, he released her hands and patted her shoulder. "How about visiting the site and then grabbing an early lunch at Molly Kate's?"

Again, without a word she nodded. "I'll get my purse."

When she left the room, he walked to the window and stared at the clouds. "Toby, I'm going to need your help, buddy."

The sun broke through so bright he had to look away.

"I'm ready."

He turned to Lexi. "Okay, partner. Let's go."

Glancing behind him he gave a covert thumbs up and mouthed, "Thanks, man."

****

When Sid suggested that he bring dinner to the house and share Toby stories, well, all I can say is that my mind stuttered. I was going to say, "No, it just isn't a good time." But the words wouldn't come, until I heard myself say, "Okay."

While lunching at Molly Kate's, I found myself studying Sid. When Toby was on my bad list and I was involved with Nate, I still felt an attraction to Sid. His laid-back personality, ready laugh, sincere interest in others, was something I'd never seen in either Nathan or Toby. Well, that is, until Toby's last few months of life. And Sid was handsome. Very handsome, both in body and soul.

Toby didn't age well. But we had history and that filtered his balding head and aging body through a soft lens in my mind. Nate was also very good looking, but, like his last name, in a wolfish, roguish sort of way.

But Sid, with thick, snow-white waves. Gentle smile. Blue eyes…

"Lex?"

I snapped to attention. "Oh." I waved a weak dismissal. "Sorry. I guess I was lost in thought about…about the boutique furniture."

"Lady, you are one committed project manager."

If only he knew…

He angled his head. "I was asking what you wanted for supper tonight."

I thought a minute. "Chinese sounds good."

"Chinese it is." He grinned. "Wine?"

"Red."

"Done. I'll be over around six-thirty."

We walked back to the office and I went to the lady's room. When I passed the full-length mirror, I caught my reflection. My clothes hung on me. My stringy hair stayed in a messy bun. Dark circles made crescents in the dull skin under my eyes. Why hadn't I noticed this?

While I admired Sid across the table at lunch, he was looking at the equivalent of a red-headed zombie. I glanced at my watch and wondered if David could work me in? I punched his number on my phone.

"Hi, stranger." The sound of chatter in the salon's background dampened my hopes. David's voice softened. "How are you?"

"David, is there *any chance* you could work me in?"

"Like today?"

"Like now."

"Well…" He paused a minute. "If you aren't in any hurry, I can work on you between customers."

"Great. When can I come?"

"Give me forty-five."

I hung up. That gave me just enough time to stop by Birdie's shop to find something that fit. On my way out, I called Avalee. She always had the latest and greatest in beauty aids.

"Hey, girl. What's up?"

"Hey. Listen, I need your help."

"Sure, anything."

"I just looked in a mirror and some stranger looked back at me, and she's a hot mess. I'm on my way to David's to get my hair done and wonder if you have something to hide my black eyes and smooth out this sandpaper skin."

"You bet I do." The relief in her voice bothered me. "Call me when you leave David and I'll meet you at your house."

"I won't have much time. Sid is bringing over dinner at six-thirty."

"Oooh."

"No, it's not like that. We are two friends reminiscing about Toby. But honestly, I do feel like I've woken up from a coma. A grief coma."

"I'm so glad to hear that. We've all been worried about you but didn't want to say anything. Molly Kate has been about to bust. She said she was giving you one more month and then she was going to drive you to a therapist herself."

"It's been hard. You know how it is to lose someone. But on top of everything, I feel so guilty for the years I spent hating him. All that time…wasted."

Avalee was quiet for a moment. "You know? Maybe that is why it worked out for him to come and live with you. I mean, if you think about it, that whole situation was so strange, them letting him out of prison on compassionate release and him having no place to go."

"You have a point."

"Yeah. So don't go muddying that up with self-condemnation."

"Thanks, sugar. You're right. Toby didn't want that for me, and I think…no…I know he would be happy that Sid is coming over."

"Okay then, sweet-pea. I'll be over with a slew of cosmetic magic as soon as you get home."

"Thanks, hon." I clicked off the phone, smiling.

I've said this before, but Lord I loved my friends.

****

Wow. I turned this way and that admiring myself

in the mirror. No doubt about it, David was the best. My ginger tresses looked healthy and shiny. I loved the new shoulder length bob and sassy bangs. Avalee'd worked her cosmetic miracles. I was almost back to my old self. Maybe even better. I purchased a sage green sundress that fit in the bodice but flared out at the waist, making me look like I actually had a figure. Sakes, I never thought I'd worry about being too skinny.

The doorbell rang. Sid was right on time. I swung open the door and grinned. "Hi, Sid."

He stood frozen.

I motioned. "Well, don't just stand there like a piece of Miss Cladie's yard art, come on in."

He shook his head. "Man. You look…sorry, I wasn't expecting…I mean, you look amazing."

I had to admit. That reaction felt good. Stepping back, I smiled up at him. "Why, thank you, my gallant knight."

His sweet smile grew. "Tis all true, my lady."

This would be a good night. I could tell. Just as I pushed the door closed, a beam of sunlight bore down on my front porch.

Smiling, I let it warm my face and received what I knew was Toby's blessing. I could move on with life.

Sid stood behind me. He also saw the beam. "That's the second time today."

I turned with a jerk. I was so lost in the moment that I didn't notice he was anywhere nearby.

"Second?"

"Yeah." He thought a moment. "Say, why don't we have a glass of wine? I think it is time we have a serious talk."

****

We settled on the couch in the living room and Sid turned to me. "I wasn't sure when the right time would be for me to talk to you about this. But, and I know this might sound to *woo-woo* for you, but I think Toby is sending us messages.

I started to say something, but Sid held up his hand.

"The week after Christmas, Toby asked me to watch over you, and…" he paused, "to love you."

Sid let that settle between us before continuing on.

"He said he had noticed my attraction to you and asked me if I loved you."

I caught my breath and my heart hammered in anticipation of Sid's answer.

"I told him I did. And I do, Lex. I love you and have for a long time."

"Oh, Sid."

He held his hand up again. "I promised him I'd take care of you, but today I felt like I was failing my promise. The Lexi we knew and loved was withering away and I felt so helpless. Then, when you went to get your purse, I looked out the window and told Toby that I needed his help. Just after the words left my lips a beam of light broke through the clouds and I took it as a sign. And now, just as I walk in the door, it happens again. I believe it is Toby showing us that he approves."

I put my finger to his lips. "My turn. I know it's his blessing. This has happened to me too. And Toby asked me to love again, but he didn't give me a suggestion as to who." Then I remembered his warning and chuckled. "Well, actually he did. He told me the one person not to love. Nate. But he said I would figure it out. And now I know…it's you."

Sid hesitated, then leaned over and kissed me. I was expecting beams of light breaking through the window and a hallelujah chorus from angelic beings led by Toby himself. But what I got instead was a revelation of love, of promise, of a new beginning.

We spent the rest of the evening laughing and crying over our Toby memories. Being with Sid felt so right. So natural. Like coming home.

The next morning, when I met Sid for coffee before finalizing our flooring decisions, I asked him, "Sid, when did you realize you loved me?"

He threw his head back and laughed. "Since that day you tangled with old man Fleming after Avalee pitched her flower market idea. I knew you were the fire I needed."

He was right. The council meeting about our project wasn't my first rodeo with Mr. Fleming. Avalee had this great idea for a flower market to save Miss Cladie's greenhouse business that had been in her family for three generations. When the neighborhood was developed around her family home the city grandfathered in her acreage and allowed her business to continue. But when Avalee came up with the market idea, the council needed to give approval because of the large groups it would attract.

Sid laughed and shook his head, "When you passed Fleming and drilled that glare at him, threatening to write an article about that meeting, I knew you were a force to be dealt with."

"I guess I can be a little fiery."

"A little?"

"Okay, but you are the calm to my storm." I reached over and took his hand. This felt so right and yet guilt tugged at me. I mean, what kind of woman was I? In love with three men in one year? Okay, so I wasn't exactly in love with Nate. Toby was more of a renewal. Sid, he was different from Toby and Nate. He was a kindred spirit. A soulmate. Looking back, I realized that all the time we'd been working together my love for him had been growing so quietly that I didn't recognize it. But when he said he loved me, I knew I loved him too. There was only one thing I knew to do.

Go talk to Miss Cladie.

Chapter Eighteen

The circle of life has many ripples

"Knock, knock?" I stood at Miss Cladie's kitchen door and wondered how many times people had passed through this portal seeking wisdom. Even before she opened the door, I heard her call, "Get yourself in here, girl." She swung it open. "Lord, you are a sight for this old woman's sore eyes. Sugar, you look wonderful."

I walked straight into her arms. "Thank you, Miss Cladie."

"What can I get you? Coffee? I have some pound cake I can toast."

"Yes to both." I sat at her little drop-leaf table and admired the smiling fruits and vegetables on her wall. They had been there for as long as I could remember. "And I hope for some advice too."

"That I've got plenty of, don't know if it is worth much though."

She cut two thick slices of pound cake and slathered it with butter, then slipped both in her little toaster oven. While the cake toasted, she poured our coffee.

"Here ya are, hon.

She set the coffee and cake in front of me and honestly? All felt right with the world at that very minute. I bit into that slice of buttery, vanilla goodness and groaned. "This is sooo good."

"Brings back memories of you girls the morning after a sleepover."

"It does. You'd always bring this to us while we watched Saturday morning cartoons."

Miss Cladie sighed. "Seems like yesterday." She sipped her coffee then set the cup down. "Now, what is it you wanted to talk about?"

I took a deep breath. "Sid told me he loved me, and I told him I loved him too."

She clapped her hands together. "Why, that's wonderful."

"Is it, Miss Cladie? I mean, three men in one year?"

"Three? You loved Nathan?"

"Well, no. But there was something there. And before you say anything, I know it was nothing more than lust."

Miss Cladie raised her brows. "I wasn't going to say nary a word."

"You were thinking it though."

Grinning at me over her cup she quipped, "I might have been. Go on."

"But then there was Toby. I loved him, but in a different way from when we were first married. Marrying again was like shutting the door on our past problem and all its demons. Like sealing a promise for the future. And now here I am, in love, yet again. Is it wrong? Too soon? Am I just rebounding?"

Miss Cladie sat back and crossed her arms over her chest. "Toby told me that one day you would come and talk to me about Sid."

"He did?" An odd sensation of surprise tingled

inside me.

"Yes, ma'am, he did."

"What did he say?"

"It was right after y'all married and he could tell his time was near. That boy was in a tizzy for worrying over you being alone. He said he had noticed something between you and Sid when he first came, even though you were with Nathan. He felt you two were right together and would eventually find each other. So, he asked me to tell you about our conversation should you ever come to talk with me about it."

She leaned over the table and patted my hand. "This is what Toby wanted. He will rest easy now."

I couldn't stop the tears from spilling down my cheeks and neither could dear Miss Cladie. We had a good cleansing cry and another piece of toasted pound cake.

****

Sid stared at the numbers on the sheet at his desk. It was no use. Thoughts about Lexi filled his mind. She said she loved him. She. Loved. Him. He could hardly wrap his mind around her words—*her wonderful words*.

He thought of his ex-wife, Barbara. They were just out of high school when they married. A big mistake. They realized this a little less than a year after they had said their vows. The "D" word was tossed around, but then Chris came along, so they decided to try and make their marriage work. But when they had an unplanned pregnancy, Barbara was furious, fuming how it would ruin her figure. She even threatened to have an abortion, but Sid wouldn't have any part of that, and Cody was born.

The woman was never meant to have children. This was obvious by the way she treated the boys. Sid had resigned himself to a miserable marriage for their sake, but Barbara made his resolution hard.

Then, one day the school called him to say no one picked up his sons. On his way to the school, he tried to call Barbara but didn't get an answer. When they arrived home, she wasn't there. Her clothes were still in the closet. Her car was still in the garage. Only her purse was gone.

He reported her missing to the police, called her mother, her friends, even had a private detective try to find her. He worried that she had been abducted and murdered or injured and couldn't get in touch with anyone. It never crossed his mind that she would up and leave her children like that, no matter how bad a parent she was. No one heard a word from her for years until she showed up two Christmas ago.

Sid shook those unhappy thoughts from his mind and let the memory of Lexi's kiss play across his mind. From the first day she volunteered to help him with Moonlight's public relations, he'd wondered what it would be like to hold her in his arms. He'd felt a connection with her immediately. As their friendship grew, he found himself imagining her as more than a friend. When Toby came on the scene, he watched his hopes for a relationship with her fade. Then, in a whiplash moment, Toby became their cupid. It was all so bizarre. And now, she was his. She was really, actually, his.

He returned his attention to the numbers he'd been staring at and tried to make something out of it. But it was no use. Maybe he'd take a stroll. Lexi was home and she only lived four blocks away. Maybe they could work from there.

Or…maybe not.

****

I sat in my swing to enjoy the last of the cool afternoons. After all, here in the south, spring is just a suggestion before summer pounces. To my relief I spied Sid strolling down the sidewalk. Just as I waved, my phone rang. It was Avalee.

"Hey girl, what's up?"

"The baby is finally coming."

"Well, it's about time. She's what? A month overdue?"

"Three weeks. I think little Ava waited for Skye to walk in the graduation ceremony. Already a considerate child."

"Yeah, you just go on thinking that. How is Skye?

"Duff called and said she is a lot tougher than he ever thought about being."

"Good for him." I patted the seat next to me on the swing and mouthed to Sid that it was Avalee. "Are you and Ty there now?"

"Yes, and it won't be long. I just wanted to let you know."

"Call me as soon as that little princess gets here."

"I will. Bye."

I clicked off and clapped my hands. "The baby is coming."

"That's great. You want to be there?"

"I don't think so. Skye's mom is there, so are Duff's parents. Ty's son, Glen, and Cladie are there too. That's welcoming committee enough."

Sid placed his arm around my shoulder. "How

about you giving me a ride back to town? We can grab dinner. Then, if the baby comes, we can go check her out."

"Excellent idea."

I nestled against Sid and we gently swung back and forth, while listening to the cacophony of birds tweeting out their claim and defending their territory, some sang to attract and court mates. Those that found a mate were busy tearing up my hanging ferns while building nests in them. I didn't mind. It was the dance of Spring.

Sid kissed the top of my head and I gazed up at him. I couldn't explain it, but it felt like we had been a couple for years.

To me, it just seemed we were better together.

****

During dinner, I called Avalee.

"Do we have a baby yet?"

"Yes." Avalee's pitch couldn't get any higher. "She just arrived. Oh, Lex, she is beautiful."

"Of course she is." I grinned at Sid. "Mind if Sid and I pop by?"

"Come on."

Ava Elizabeth was an eight-pound bundle of joy. We all pressed our noses against the nursery's glass window trying to get a closer view. And I don't mind telling you, when they stuck that needle in her little foot, I wanted to slap someone. But Sid told me to settle down, assuring me it was an important test. Who knew? I sure didn't.

The elevator dinged and Molly Kate came bustling out of the elevator with Stan in close tow behind her.

"Where's that child?"

Ty waved. "Over here."

We all stood at the window ooohing and ahhhhing until she was taken to Skye's room. We waited on pins and needles until we were told we could go in and see her. That poor baby. When we finally got our hands on her, she was passed around like a bowl of butterbeans over the dinner table.

After we all got a turn holding her, Stan said, "Well, as is custom in the old country, let's go to the pub and wet her head."

"Sounds like a plan." Ty and Avalee hugged Skye and Duff, then we all left. When we got to the elevator Ty's phone rang.

"Hey, Dad. What's up?"

It was clear that whatever the call was about, it wasn't good. Avalee put her hand on his shoulder.

"Is it…?"

He nodded. "We need to go to Dad and Mom's."

I hurried behind them. "What's up?"

Ty sleeved his eyes. "It's Mom. She's gone"

Avalee slipped her arm around his waist. Words weren't needed. When we got to the parking lot, I hugged Ava and Ty.

The ride on the way home was quiet. I thought about death and how I'd come to view it, not as an end, but a passing. A portal into what was true life. And so was birth. Ty's mom left and his granddaughter arrived on the same day. They had exchanged places.

The circle of life goes on.

****

The next three weeks were bittersweet. Sid and I helped out all we could in the celebration and transition of life. I rarely saw Avalee or the baby and I was aching to get my hands on that little bundle.

Finally, Avalee called.

"Well, hello there, Mimi."

"Hey, girl."

"How's the new family?"

"Skye is stressing over every little thing. That child can't sneeze for Duff or her wanting to rush her to the doctor. They're both worn out."

"It's funny how a tiny, helpless, little human can turn over the proverbial fruit basket called normal life."

"That is the truth. Never having a child myself, I guess this is normal. But it seems silly to me."

"I'm in the same boat as you."

"Anyway, I'm giving Skye and Duff the morning off. Want to come over and get some baby snuggles.

"Absolutely. Sid is coming over in a bit, I'm sure he'll want some of those baby kisses too."

"Great. See y'all in a sec."

I slipped on my shoes and walked outside. Just as I stepped onto my porch, I stopped. There was a strange car in my driveway. Who on earth?

The door opened on the driver's side and Nate slid out and stood, staring at me over the roof. I was dumbstruck. What was he doing here? Why did he come?

"Hi, Red."

I was too astonished to correct him.

"Can we talk?"

Talk? What could he possibly have to say? But I nodded anyway.

He walked toward me and darned it all, he looked fabulous. Stirrings from the past swirled through my body.

"Can we go in?"

Alarms went off in my mind and I blurted, "No."

He stopped and tilted his head.

"Sorry, I didn't mean to be so blunt. But I'd rather sit on the porch."

"That's fine." He sat on the swing, probably expecting me to sit beside him. I sat in the rocker.

"Why are you here?"

"I'm stopping by on my way to that conference to see Skye and the baby. I'm still mentoring her, and we've built a good friendship."

Dare I tell him where the baby was? Nope. Instead, I asked, "But why are you *here?"* I pointed at the porch floor. "At *my* house?"

He leaned forward, propping his arms on his knees. "We didn't part on good terms."

"Well, that's an understatement if ever I heard one."

"I felt bad about that. I was wrong, Lex. It's all on me. And I wanted to apologize, face-to-face."

"Yes, you were. But…" I smiled at the thought of Sid. "It was for the best. I see that now."

He studied me for a moment, then nodded. "You look good."

"Thanks. So do you." The little devil on my shoulder prompted me to ask about Miss Breathy Voice. I tried to resist—until I couldn't, "How's Monica?"

Nate looked down and shook his head. "I wish *I* could say it was all for the best, too. But I can't." He glanced up at me and sighed. "She's…" He thought a moment. "Turns out, she's a spoiled daddy's girl."

He sat up and raked his fingers through his hair. "I'm having to walk a thin line working for her father and pleasing her. Sometimes, I'm not sure if it is worth it after all."

I nodded sympathetically on the outside, but on the inside, I thought, *serves you right.*

He gave me that half-smile that used to set me on fire and said, "I could use a little southern comfort now and then."

Talk about ice water hitting me dead on in the face.

"Get off my porch."

He splayed his hands. "What?"

"You heard me." I stood and pointed my finger toward the driveway. "Get off my porch and into that car and leave."

"Lex, baby. I didn't mean what you are thinking. I was just asking for us to occasionally have a drink and conversation."

Just then Sid pulled up to the curb and jumped out of his car. "Lexi? Are you okay?"

"I will be when he leaves."

The ever gentle, ever patient Sid walked onto the porch and slipped his arm around me.

"It was nice seeing you, Nate." He pulled me close. "But Lexi and I have plans."

Nate looked at me, then Sid, then back at me. Understanding dawned on his face. He shoved his hands into his pockets and nodded.

"Nice seeing you both again." Nate rocked on his feet a few seconds, then looked up at me. "Lexi, I *am* sorry. Really, I am. About everything. You are a wonderful woman." He glanced at Sid. "And you, my friend, are a lucky man."

He turned, strode to his car, got in, and drove off.

Sid turned and stood in front of me. Just before he

kissed me, he whispered, "I'm a lucky man indeed."

****

That evening my encounter with Nate still had me pretty shaken. As the saying goes, I dodged a bullet with that man.

Sid kissed me, then said, "A penny for your thoughts."

I laid my head on his shoulder and said, "The price has gone up."

"Oh? What is it now?"

"A glass of wine."

"Wine it is. Be right back."

Sid returned and handed me a glass of Syrah.

"Okay, paid in full. Now, your thoughts?"

"I was thinking about Nate. If Toby had not come back into my life and helped me to trust love again, I might be stuck with that jerk."

Sid brought my hand to his lips and kissed it. "If Toby never taught me to hope, I might not be sitting next to you now."

"I'm glad he did."

Companionable silence enveloped us as the tree frogs and katydids began to sing their songs in the twilight. I let out a contented sigh. "You'd never get this in Manhattan."

"No." Sid nuzzled my neck "I love you Lexi Lowe."

"And I love you, Sid Campbell."

He lowered his lips onto mine in a slow, tender, kiss. And I knew, just like this kiss, would be how our relationship would develop. Slow and tender.

Chapter Nineteen

One year later…January 31st

The morning felt unusually warm for the last day of January. I was grateful. On this day last year I came to this very spot, Toby's memorial bench by the duck pond, and gathered my thoughts before releasing his ashes to the wind. I remember being chilled through.

Today I stared off at the brown grass, the naked trees lifting their branches into the cloudless blue sky and thought of him. One year ago he broke free of his body and went to his eternal home. Even though he wasn't physically with me, his impact on my life remained. The same was true for all who knew and loved him.

Sid sat beside me lost in his own world of thought. We decided to come to this place together and say thank you to Toby. After all, this was his highest hope for me. To find someone who would love me for the rest of my life. Toby chose Sid. He was an insightful man.

Sid shifted on the bench, lifted his face and smiled. Tears ran from the corners of his eyes and down the sides of his face. He took a deep breath and blew it out.

"Toby, my friend, because of you I am the most blessed man on earth. Today, I am going to keep the promise I made to you."

I watched as Sid slid off the bench onto one knee. “Lexi, I want us to spend the rest of our lives together, living, loving, creating. You are my kindred spirit, my soulmate, my best friend. Will you be my wife?”

The breeze picked up freeing a dried maple leaf from a nearby tree. It dropped onto my lap. I smiled. Toby’s reminder of starting over. I looked into Sid’s eyes.

“Yes.” I leaned over and kissed him. “Oh, yes.”

He stood, raised me to my feet, and held me close. This moment was not like any I’d ever experienced. The fullness of presence, of peace, of absolute joy, took my breath away. And then…

Sid stepped back and reached into his pocket, then held up a simple platinum solitaire.

I drew in a breath. It was beautiful. I held my hand up and he slid it onto my finger. The sun glinted and winked off the diamond. It made me think that Toby was there laughing. I grinned and spoke to the field where we stood. “Thank you, Toby.”

We walked hand-in-hand back to Miss Cladie’s where she and the girls prepared lunch. We planned on spending the afternoon together telling Toby stories. Well, I had the best one to tell.

****

I stared at myself in the mirror, a sixty-year-old woman dressed in white—again. Even so, it felt right. This was a new beginning. I was a new person. Sid and I loved each other in the deepest, purest, soul-to-soul way. Yes, this was right.

In the background were snatches of conversation and giggles from the best friends a girl could ever have. Molly Kate went all out decorating the B & B’s back terrace. Sid and I wanted to keep things simple, and for once, Molly Kate agreed.

Jema secured my flower crown with pins, and Molly Kate handed me my bouquet of white peonies picked from Miss Cladie's garden.

Avalee straightened the train of my Boho gown. "It's time." Her eyes glittered, threatening my own tears.

The string quartet played while guests were seated. With Sid being the mayor, we had to keep the guest list for the wedding to a minimum limiting it to family, close friends, and of course the town council. But not so for the reception. Stan and Molly Kate were going all out. I could hardly wait.

"Hey, baby girl, are you ready?" Miss Cladie dabbed her eyes with her lace-edged hanky. "You look beautiful."

My eyes teared up. "Now, don't you go crying Cladie Mae, or you'll start me up."

She led me up the aisle to Sid. Oh my goodness. The only thought that kept running through my mind was what had I done to deserve him. He held his hand out to me. I drank in the sight of him, so distinguished in his black tux. I loved his thick hair and imagined running my fingers through those soft, white, waves. His steady gaze at me with his impossibly blue eyes made me giddy anticipation. I took his hand and there we vowed our lives to each other—forever.

****

Our reception was beyond extravagant and wonderful. Stan did himself proud. His buffet offered roasted pig, smoked brisket, shrimp and grits, roasted rosemary potatoes, corn on the cob, fried okra, fried tempura asparagus—yes, fried—hey, we are in the south where everything is fried, even butter. And, as a nod to the health conscious, there were six salad choices. Dessert was an array of cakes. Carrot, my fave. Also Miss Cladie's coconut cake and her eight layer golden vanilla cake iced with dark chocolate buttercream. I planned on eating a slice of each.

The delicious aromas drove me wild. But having to shake the hands of every citizen of Moonlight took a while.

Ty snapped so many pictures it would take a month for us to go through them. Ty did what he did best, shooting photos that told a story.

What a celebration. We ate like it was our last supper, toasted with champagne, and true to my plan, I sampled some of all the cakes, refusing to feel one whit bad about it. This was a special day when calories didn't count. And you know? Even if they did, I took care of those little fat-producing demons by dancing until twilight to big band music.

After hours of dancing and mingling with guests, I needed a quiet moment to myself and to reflect. I left Sid to visit with his boys and went to the library. When I swung open the door I startled an old gentleman sitting in the leather chair by the fire. *He was smoking a pipe*. Ah ha! I caught him.

"Oh, sorry, sir. Don't let me bother you." I put my hand out. "Just stay where you are." He smiled and nodded, not saying a word.

I closed the door feeling pretty smug. Molly Kate walked toward me pushing a cart of dirty dishes. I waved her down.

"I caught him."

She frowned. "Caught who?"

"The pipe smoker. In the library. He's an old gentleman, looks to be in his late eighties, or early nineties."

"But we don't have any guests that age."

"Maybe he's a wedding guest, a local who sneaks in. I don't know. We opened the reception to the entire town."

Molly flattened her lips. "Well, whoever he is, he isn't welcome to smoke."

She barged in the room. "Sir…."

Stopping, she looked around. The room was empty. The only evidence he had been there was the fragrant pipe smoke and the spicy smell of mint.

I stared at where he had sat and then at MK.

"Impossible," I said, stabbing my finger toward the chair. "He was right there."

"Maybe he slipped out while you weren't looking."

"But I just stepped away enough to flag you down in the hall."

"I don't know, but he's gone now." She put her arm around my waist. "Hey, let's not let this distract you from what is the best day of your life."

I turned and looked back into the room, then at Molly Kate.

"You're right."

We returned to the reception and I walked straight into Sid's arms. Looking up at him I smiled and whispered, "Wanna go honeymoon?"

He lifted his eyebrows and a slow smile crept across his handsome face. "Yes, ma'am."

And just like that old man, we slipped out the door and into our new life together.

Epilogue

This new year looks promising. Jema and Levi are moving back soon. I can hardly wait. Another *great* thing is that Sid's son, Chris, and his wife are expecting again. You know what that means? I'm going to be a grandma. I'm finally having a baby, well, sort of. I'm already thinking of grandma names. What do you think of "precious?" Wouldn't it be great to be called precious all day long?

Oh, and that mystery man smoking a pipe at Molly Kate's bed and breakfast has never been seen again. But the pipe smoke still comes and goes. I'm wondering if Stan is behind all of this. Maybe it is his little prank to drive Molly Kate crazy. Sort of his passive-aggressive pay back for all the bossiness of his beloved wife.

Or, maybe, *just maybe*, the house is really haunted.

Who knows?

MOLLY KATE'S STUFFED DATES

Ingredients:

18 (1 by 1/4-inch) pieces cream cheese
18 pitted dates (preferably Medjool)
6 slices bacon cut crosswise into thirds

Instructions:

Heat the oven to 400 degrees
Stuff 1 piece of cheese into each date
Wrap one piece of bacon around each date and secure bacon with a toothpick
Arrange dates, bacon seam down and 1 inch apart in a shallow baking pan.
Bake 5 minutes, then turn dates over with tongs and bake until bacon is crisp, 5 to 6 minutes more.
Drain on a paper towel

MISS CLADIE'S DECADENT COCONUT CAKE

Ingredients

Cake:

3 cups cake flour

1 Tbsp baking powder

1/2 tsp salt

1/8 tsp cream of tartar

2 cups granulated sugar

3/4 cup unsalted butter, at room temperature

1/4 cup vegetable oil

1 1/3 cups unsweetened canned coconut milk

2 large eggs, yolks and whites separated

4 large egg whites, at room temperature

1 tsp coconut extract

1/2 tsp vanilla extract

Coconut Cream (such as Coco López. I usually find it in the cocktail mixers section)

Frosting:

12 oz cream cheese, at room temperature

3/4 cup butter, at room temperature

1 tsp coconut extract

5 cups powdered sugar

2 cups shredded coconut

Instructions

Cake:

Preheat oven to 350 degrees. Grease 3 9-inch round cake pans, line the bottom with a circular piece of parchment, and set pans aside.

Sift cake flour into a large mixing bowl, then add baking powder and salt and whisk mixture.

Whip 6 egg whites with cream of tartar on medium-high speed until stiff (but not dry) peaks form and scrape into separate bowl, set aside.

Blend together granulated sugar, butter and oil until well combined. (I use a stand mixer with a paddle attachment) Scrape down bowl

Add in egg yolks one at a time and mix until combined after each addition (reserve 2 egg whites), then mix in coconut and vanilla extracts. Scrape down bowl.

Add 1/3 of the flour mixture, blend just until combined. Add half of the coconut milk, mix just until combined. Mix in another 1/3 of the flour mixture followed by remaining coconut milk. Finish by mixing in last 1/3 of the flour mixture.

Using a rubber spatula, carefully fold 1/3 of the egg whites into cake batter at a time and fold just combined after each addition (don't over-mix and deflate egg whites).

Divide batter among prepared cake pans. Spread batter into an even layer and bake in preheated oven until toothpick inserted into center of cake comes out clean, about 19 - 22 minutes.

While cakes are warm, (and still in their pans) poke each layer with a fork or skewer.

Pour over each layer with coconut cream and let it soak in.

Put layers in the refrigerator a couple of hours and let them get completely cool. If you make this cake ahead of time, it is fine to leave them in there overnight. Cooling them makes the layers easier to handle when frosting.

When you are ready to frost the layers, take a thin knife and run it around the edge. Set the bottom of the pan in hot water for a minute or two and then flip it onto a flat surface.

Remove parchment and if the top is domed, gentle cut a thin slice off with a serrated knife to level it out.

Put the first layer on the cake plate and frost the top. Add another layer and frost the top. Add the last layer and frost top and sides.

Gently press shredded coconut cake evenly on sides to adhere.

Frosting:

Whip butter with cream cheese until smooth and fluffy. Mix in coconut extract. Add powdered sugar and whip on medium speed with a whisk attachment until smooth and fluffy.

LEXI'S SAUSAGE BALLS

Ingredients:

3 cups Bisquick mix
1 pound uncooked bulk pork sausage
4 cups shredded Cheddar cheese (16 ounces)
1/2 cup grated Parmesan cheese
1/2 cup milk
1/2 teaspoon dried rosemary leaves, crushed
1 1/2 teaspoons chopped fresh parsley or 1/2 teaspoon parsley flakes
Barbecue sauce or chili sauce, if desired

Instructions:

Heat oven to 350°F.
Lightly grease bottom and sides of 15x10x1-inch pan.
In large bowl, stir together all ingredients except barbecue sauce, using hands or spoon.
Shape mixture into 1-inch balls.
Place in pan.
Bake 20 to 25 minutes or until brown.
Immediately remove from pan.
Serve warm with sauce for dipping.

TOBY'S PROPER BRITISH SHANDY

Ingredients:

Your favorite beer or lager
Your favorite lemon-lime soda

Instructions:

Pour half of each beverage slowly into beer glasses. If you are making it by the pitcherful, use equal parts of both.

Note: The difference between shandy in England and the US is a matter of misinterpretation. In England, soft drinks such as 7-Up or Sprite are referred to as "lemonade." Naturally, those of us in the US thought that meant what we call lemonade, therefore the two ways to make shandy.

A word about the author…

Linda Apple writes from her soul and speaks from her heart.

Her novels, *The Women of Washington Avenue* and *Avalee's Gift*, are born from years of living in the South and loving southern culture, people, and of course the deep friendships forged over the years.

She is also a children's author. Her book, *BOWWOW~Book of Winston's Words of Wisdom* is inspired by her Scotty Winston and his view of the world.

Her nonfiction books include *Writing Life~Your Stories Matter* and *Writing from Your Soul*. She has been published in 16 *Chicken Soup for the Soul* book series.

She is a public speaker and teaches workshops for writers' conferences nationwide. Besides writing, her passion is to help others succeed in their writing goals.

Linda and her husband, Neal, live in Rogers, AR close to their five children, four children-in-law, and thirteen grandchildren.

You can visit with Linda at:

http://lindaapple.com

Thank you for purchasing
this publication of The Wild Rose Press, Inc.

For questions or more information
contact us at
info@thewildrosepress.com.

The Wild Rose Press, Inc.
www.thewildrosepress.com

www.ingramcontent.com/pod-product-compliance
Lightning Source LLC
Chambersburg PA
CBHW060548260626
47161CB00003B/1111